BUTTERFLY KISSES

A Novel by

Judith P. Vaughan

This entire book is a work of fiction. Names, places, and characters are either product of the author's imagination or used fictitiously. Any resemblance to actual events or locales or persons, living or dead, is entirely coincidental.

No vampires were harmed in the writing of this book.

BUTTERFLY KISSES

Copyright @2011 by Judith P. Vaughan

Cover and art copyright @2011 by Judith P. Vaughan

http://www.judithpvaughan.com

To the memory of my mother, Delia.

I miss you.

BUTTERFLY KISSES

CHAPTER 1

It was another boring cold afternoon in a week of dull and depressing rain. The type of weather you would like to cozy up with a book.

I had just finished reading Anna Karenina for the umpteenth time. The pages in this old book were coming apart. I was in desperate need of something new to read, something exciting to keep my mind out of those self-destructive thoughts I have been having lately.

I waited on the couch for my mother to come home from work and take me to the bookstore. She had promised me I could buy a couple of new books if I got all A's on my report card, and I did. I would go by myself, but it has been raining all day, besides I had to depend on my mother to take me everywhere, she was my means of transportation. It really sucked not having my driver's permit and just thinking about it, depressed me more. I sighed.

The minutes past and she was not home yet.

Succumbed with boredom, I stared out the window and counted the raindrops as they slowly slid down the window glass. My breath fogged up the glass and I drew a heart on the window. As the moisture faded from the window, the image of the house across the street seemed to appear slowly, right in the middle of the heart, just like a mirage in the oasis.

This house across from ours stood out from the rest, it was relatively larger and contemporary, unlike the smaller colonial style houses in the neighborhood. The house had been vacant for a long time, and I could understand why.

I smiled, and suddenly found myself daydreaming.

"A penny for your thoughts," My mother said, and sat down next to me on the couch.

I snapped out of my daze and I smiled, "Hi, mom, I didn't hear you come in."

She chuckled, "Yes, I noticed. What are you staring at?" She gently touched my hair.

"I think we have new neighbors."

"Do you mean that mansion across the street?" She looked out the window.

"Yes, the sign is gone ---and I saw a car parked outside last night."

"Are you spying on people again?"

"I wasn't spying--- I was asleep already when the noise woke me up and I went to see what was going on, ---it was kind of weird actually, I saw their moving van but never saw anyone, just kept hearing noises."

"Ok... and what's wrong with that?" My mother frowned.

"Nothing, —just that it was very peculiar seeing someone move in the middle of the…" I stopped when I noticed the car pulling up the driveway of the huge house. "Look mom here they come, that's the car I saw last night," I kneeled on the couch and faced the window to get a better view.

My mom looked out the window again, "Ok Amber, stop snooping, they seem like decent people to me, ---I'm sure they had a reason for moving at such a late hour."

A nice looking couple dressed in classy trendy clothes stepped out of the car and entered the house.

I kept staring at the house, "Really mom? You don't find that a bit odd?"

"Well…" She said with a little strain in her voice.

"Aha!" I turned to her, "They are probably weirdoes wanted by the FBI, right?" I said amused.

She chuckled, "Hmm, I wouldn't go to that extreme?" She

paused and pondered.

I could see her expression changing as she tried to make sense of it. I knew if she thought that creeps had moved in our neighborhood she would keep an eye on them since she belonged to the neighborhood watch.

"Ok, let's put an end to your curiosity. I'll bake a fresh batch of cookies and we'll take them to our new neighbors, that way you can take a better look. How does that sound?" She schemed and winked at me.

"Sounds as corny as an episode of Desperate Housewives, but I'm in," I smiled and winked back. I knew she was curious too.

Later, I noticed two other expensive cars parked in the driveway that I had not seen before.

"Amber, come help me, please," My mother shouted. Her voice echoed from inside the kitchen.

"I'm coming."

Minutes later, while the cookies baked in the oven, I walked outside and sat on the front porch to wait. A cold breeze hit my face. I tucked my hands inside the sleeves of my oversized sweater.

The rain had stopped, but the smell of the rain lingered, filling the chilly air with its aroma.

A few minutes later, my mother came out holding a small basket full of cookies. She had wrapped the cookies nicely in pink plastic and placed them inside the basket.

"Are you ready?" She asked.

"Yes."

We crossed the street, stepping over the small puddles of water that remained on the pavement.

I stared at the two cars parked on the driveway. I noticed that tiny water bubbles from the rain covered the cars, the water bubbles sparkled like little gems on top of the brand new shiny cars.

We got to the front door of the house and my mother rang the doorbell.

I stood next to my mother. I was excited and scared to meet the new neighbors.

Then a tall, handsome man in his mid-forties opened the door. He had light ivory skin and brown hair.

"Yes, may I help you?" He greeted us with a smile.

"Hi, I'm Savannah Ross and this is my daughter, Amber. We

live across the street and we just wanted to welcome you and your family to the neighborhood," My mother smiled, and handed him the small basket with the freshly baked cookies.

Then the man shifted his eyes to me and smiled, "come on in, I'll introduce you to my wife--- I'm Aubrey Cromwell by the way," he held the door open as we walked in.

I followed my mother inside the house and we stood on the large bright foyer with high ceilings, the room was very cold to the point that I could see my warm breath in it. The shiny tiled floor and elaborated staircase with black wrought iron railings gave the room a grand palace style welcome.

A very attractive woman with brownish red hair and fair skin walked out of the living room and into the foyer.

"This is my wife, Estella," Mr. Cromwell said.

My mother reached across to shake her hand, "Hi nice to meet you, I'm Savannah and this is my daughter, Amber. We live across the street from you."

"It's nice to meet you both," she turned to me, "---your name is Amber?"

"Yes ma'am," I answered.

Estella repeated my name again, she then quirked one eyebrow and turned her glance to her husband.

"Yes, her name is Amber, sweetheart," Mr. Cromwell nodded his head and had a delightful grin on his face.

I then quickly glanced at my mom and gave her an inquisitive look, wondering if the woman was hard of hearing.

My mom shrugged her shoulders and kept a straight face.

"Nice to meet you, Amber," Estella smiled.

I gave her a pleasant smile, but I was laughing in the inside. Not only the beautiful woman was hard of hearing but a little slow too, I thought.

"Nice to meet you, ma'am," I shook her hand.

Her delicate hand was soft and smooth, but extremely cold.

I swiftly pulled my hand away and smiled politely. I glanced around checking out the inside of their enormous house. "You have a very nice house," I said to her.

"Thank you. ---I hope this is not the last time we see you here."

I smiled timidly and turned to my mom.

"They brought us cookies," Mr. Cromwell handed the basket to Estella.

"Oh... how wonderful, that is very sweet of you, thank you," Estella smiled.

A young man appeared at the top of the elaborated stairwell. He was tall with a slim built. He then proceeded to walk down the stairs; his steps were slow and cautious, creating a sense of mystery about him. He then stopped and looked to where we were standing.

I do not think he had noticed that we were standing there, because he seemed surprised to see us. I got chills when I saw his face. I could hear my heart pounding, it sounded like wild horses galloping. I do not know if it was for good or bad reasons, but he made me feel uncomfortable especially when he looked at me. I had seen him before but it was not in person. It was in one of my recurring delusional dreams, one of those that you want to forget. Small portions of that crazy dream flashed inside my head. I remembered that in the dream, I was dead and he was looking for me.

"Victor, come meet our neighbors," Estella motioned him to come.

On his way down, I felt like running away, but I did not.

He approached us and stood in front of us.

"This is our son, Victor," Estella said.

Victor also had dark brown hair and light ivory skin, beautiful hazel eyes, with a shifty mysterious gaze. He was remarkably handsome, I noticed. He was slim but physically fit, his firmed abs showed through the grey v-neck fitted shirt he was wearing. He was about my age perhaps a little bit older.

Then I saw him smile, and I felt like I could not breathe.

"This is Savannah and her daughter, ---Amber," Estella grinned.

She used her hands to display me as if I was an exhibit, and that made me feel even more uncomfortable.

My mom cleared her throat, "It's a pleasure to meet you, Victor," she shook his hand.

"The pleasure is mine," Victor answered in a serene tone. He looked at me and continued, "Hi Amber." He said softly, and tried to make eye contact with me.

I gulped when I heard him say my name. It sounded like a

beautiful melody in the wind, but still I did not want to look at him. I glanced down at the floor to avoid staring at him straight in the eyes, but I could feel his eyes glued on me, waiting for me to answer him.

His voice echoed in my head, overlapping the sound of my pounding heart. For some reason, I wanted to escape his presence, I wanted to run and hide, but my feet were getting heavier and heavier, I felt as if the tiled floor had turned into quicksand, and I was sinking with no one to save me.

"Are you ok, Amber?" Mr. Cromwell asked.

"Uhm, ---yeah," I nodded and immediately turned to my mom. "Mom, can we go, please?" I said urgently.

"Sure honey," she glanced at me concerned.

Before fleeing, I took a quick look at Victor again. I wanted to make sure my head was not playing tricks on me, and unfortunately, it was not. Victor looked exactly like the guy that had appeared in my dream.

After seeing my ungracious and horrid reaction, Victor gave me a cold and disappointed look.

"Mom, now!" I muttered. I could feel a knot in my throat as I tried to swallow. I grabbed her arm and tugged on it like a little child throwing a tantrum.

"Sorry we need to go, if you guys need anything, we are right across the street," My mother said hurriedly, as I rushed her out the front door.

I ran across the street and went to my room leaving my mother behind.

My mother finally caught up with me upstairs. "What is wrong with you today?" She asked in a chiding tone.

"Nothing..." I said with slight annoyance.

"That was very rude of you," she sounded upset.

"Sorry," I said in a more pleasant tone.

"You looked like you had seen a ghost when that boy came to say hello. Do you know him?"

"No, I don't."

"He is very cute," she smiled as she tried to get me to talk.

I shrugged and did not respond.

"They seem like nice folks, very polite and friendly," she said.

"So they seem," I mumbled.

"Don't tell me you still think they are freaks?"

"Well, didn't you hear them repeating my name over and over, as if they had never heard of it before?"

"Maybe your name reminds them of someone, ---who knows?"

"Sure, ---someone they killed." I said scornfully.

She shook her head. "Oh come on."

"It's true."

She huffed, "I'll leave you alone. I don't have time for this... I didn't raise you to be judgmental, especially when you have no reasons to be ---or do you? It has to do with that boy, doesn't it?"

"I don't want to talk about it..."

"Fine, ---but if you change your mind, I'll be downstairs using the computer."

I sighed and paused before answering, "Sure."

My mother looked disappointed and upset; she then walked to the door and glanced at me. I thought I heard her ask me something but my mind had already wandered away, everything seemed surreal; how could I dream about someone that I have never met before in my life.

After a long pause, she said in a harsh and louder tone, "Well? Aren't you going to answer me? Did you do your laundry?"

"Uhm, no ---I mean yeah, I did my laundry earlier this morning." I said confused as I came back out of the daze.

"Good," she said and locked the door behind her.

The rain started again.

I could hear the raindrops hitting the window. I laid back and stared at the ceiling, trying to figure out if I had been hallucinating, but then my eyelids started to get heavier and I fell asleep.

Later, the sound of the doorbell woke me up from my nap.

"I'll get it," My mother shouted.

A few minutes later, I heard my mom call my name.

"Amber."

"Coming mom," I answered in a dull tone and stretched as I got up from the bed. I walked unenergetically down the stairs. I combed my messy hair with my fingers, I was still felling a little drowsy from my nap. As I reached the last couple of steps, I looked up and I saw him standing by the front door with my mother.

"Hi," Victor smiled.

Again, I had the urge to flee, but my mother pulled me by the arm. I was now standing in front of him, staring at his hypnotic hazel eyes and kissable lips.

"Victor has a few questions —I told him you might be able to help him," My mother said and gave me a cunning look.

"Thanks mom." I uttered and squinted with sneer back at her.

She grinned, "I'll be in the kitchen," she said to us and when she passed by me, she whispered, "You're welcome."

I shook my head. I could not believe what she had done, —that was definitely not cool. I watched my mother walk back to the kitchen.

I puffed irritated by his presence, and immediately thought of a way to get rid of him, a little hostility would do the trick. I grinned shrewdly and put my hands in the back pockets of my faded jeans and slowly turned to Victor, "So, ---what do you want to know?"

"Like I was telling your mother, since we are new in town I thought you might be able to tell me like where are the good places to hang out? You know, ---like fun things to do at night."

I scoffed, "If you wanted the social nightlife, why didn't you move to a bigger city?"

He grinned, "I didn't mean only at night, ---of course, I also meant places to go during the day."

"We only have one mall and it's not very big. Let see there are restaurants, fast food places and coffee shops." I paused to take a quick breath before continuing, "as to hanging places, it depends on what you like, but the weirdoes hang on the street corners," I smirked. "Does that answer your question?" I rolled my eyes.

He smiled. He seemed to find amusing my sarcasm. "That's not what I asked Ms. Yellow Pages," he chuckled.

My eyes widened, "Excuse me?"

"Sorry, it's just that the way you were talking to me ---never mind," he shook his head and continued in a slow mocking tone, "Ok answer me this, when you go out with your friends where do you normally go?"

"I'm not stupid you know. I got what you were saying the first time---I just don't want to answer you." I said irritated.

"My apologies, I didn't mean to offend you, please forgive me," he paused and waited for a reaction or answer from me, his eyes calling mine.

I had no choice but to stare back deep into his eyes, as I stood there silently without a comeback.

He grinned and asked again breaking the stare competition, "So where do you and your friends hang out?"

"I don't waste my time hanging around —I have better things to do."

"Like what?"

"It's none of your business."

He chuckled, "Ok, I see this is not going anywhere." He scoffed, "Well do you at least go to Lexington High?"

"Yes." I answered snippily.

"Great! It's the same one I'm going to, maybe you can show me around the campus."

His presumptuousness made me chuckle. Dream on buddy, I thought to myself.

He smiled with mischief, he seemed to be stalling but then he asked me how old I was.

I rolled my eyes again annoyed by his game of twenty questions. I pressed my lips together, his presence had gone from frightening to annoying. Then I said with a sigh of irritation, "Why do you want to know how old I am?"

"I was just wondering because you look kind a young to be a senior," he commented.

I scoffed, "I'm a sophomore, and like I said earlier, it's none of your business."

"Sorry, I'm just trying to make friends. ---I thought since we're neighbors we could become friends, but I guess that won't be the case," he seemed to sense my contemptuousness, and continued in a bitter tone, "just curious, is everyone in town as unfriendly and rude as you are?"

His words hit me hard, even though I knew I was behaving like a rotten little brat. I do not know why I cared what he thought of me, but somehow I did. Then a feel of guilt overwhelmed me and I put myself in his place, so I answered him. "I'm almost sixteen."

He frowned, "Almost sixteen?" He gave me a crooked smile.

"Yes--- my birthday is in a few weeks." I smiled slightly, trying not to act too friendly since I did not want him to prolong his unwanted visit.

He then offered to give me a ride to school tomorrow, but I declined his offer and told him my mom would not let me, which it was the truth.

He reached for the door and said goodnight.

I felt relieved that he was leaving finally, but I had a dull sensation of sadness creeping inside me.

He turned around to face me, his hazel eyes staring back. He had an expression of defeat on his face as he exited out the door.

Then I could feel my mom's censorious eyes poking holes on the back of my head, I turned to the kitchen and I was right, I saw her standing by the doorway with her arms crossed in front of her staring right at me.

I knew I was in trouble. I twisted my mouth in dislike of what I was about to do and took a few steps forward, "wait Victor."

He turned around, "yes, Amber."

The sound of his voice saying my name, made my heart beat faster but also sent chills down my spine.

"Uhm ---a good place to hang out is the Valley Grille, they have pool tables and a bowling alley next door, ---and the food is not as bad as some say," I smiled slightly.

"Thanks," his eyes shined with a smile that would make anyone's heart melt and regretfully it did it to mine.

"Oh, and I almost forgot, ---on most Saturdays someone from school is having a party down by the lake, but you will probably hear about it when they do… those can be fun too," I said more enthusiastic.

"Thanks for the info —I'll see you at school."

"Yeah, see you later," I gave him a lazy smile and I closed the door behind him.

"Did you apologize?" My mother said startling me.

I jumped up in the air, "geez mom!" I turned around, "no I didn't."

"Why not?"

"Because, ---he didn't come for an apology."

She snickered, "he just wanted to talk to you, didn't he?"

I scoffed, "I guess, but it felt more like an interview, where do I go, what I do?"

She shook her head listening to me ramble, "so, —were you polite to him at least?"

I slurred my words, "yes, mother."

"That's my girl."

I paid close attention to my mom when the light hit her face; she was not wearing any make up and I noticed her pasty skin and dark circles under her eyes.

"Mom, are you ok?"

"I… I'm ok sweetie," she stuttered a little.

From her expression, I could see she was hiding something from me.

"You don't look ok to me. When do you go back to the doctor?"

She sighed, "my appointment is tomorrow."

"Why didn't you tell me?" I reproached.

"I don't have to tell you everything; I'm the mom in this house."

"But still, it concerns me too…" I paused a moment to gain courage to talk about her illness. "Mom, I'm scared. What if the cancer is back?" I hugged her.

"We will deal with it, besides we don't know for sure yet," she smiled softly and kissed my forehead.

I hated the thought of her going through chemotherapy again; it was so painful to see her that way. My eyes welled up with tears.

"Don't you dare start crying," She took a deep breath, and forced a smile, "why don't you go to bed, tomorrow is a school day."

"I love you mom," I kissed her on the cheek. I could see the apprehension in her eyes.

"I love you too. --- I'll be upstairs in a minute, ---go on," she patted me on the butt.

I stopped in the middle of the stairs and turned, "Mom, do you think tomorrow you can take me to get a new book?"

"I'm sorry honey, I forgot, but tomorrow I'll take you, — I promise."

I grinned, "thanks mom," I headed to my room and changed to my sleepwear. I stood in front of the mirror brushing my hair.

Then my mother walked in, "let me help you with that," she said and took the brush away from my hand and started to brush my hair ever so gently. "Do you remember the pigtails you liked so much when you were little?"

I chuckled, "yes, I remember."

She continued brushing my hair and styled my hair in pigtails, "your hair is getting so long, are you going to get it cut?"

"Nah —I kind of like it long."

She turned me around to face her and she hugged me tightly.

"Mom, you are crushing me," I whined.

"You look like my little baby."

"What are you talking about; I am still your little baby," I said with a grin.

"Yes you are, but you're almost a woman, ---and a very beautiful one too," she touched my face, "you have seem to have caught Victor's interest, ---I saw how he was looking at you."

"No, he is not," I said aloofly and walked to my bed.

"Oh sure… I think he got your attention too, ---he is very handsome."

"Mom," I complained.

She chuckled, "There is nothing wrong with feeling attracted to someone, especially someone that looks like him. I was young once too, exactly about your age, when I fell for your dad…"

I interrupted. "Mom, I don't want to hear about you and my dad, please."

"I know honey, ---but I was exactly your age when we did it."

"Mom!" I covered my ears.

"I just don't want you to make the same mistake I did. I want you to wait to have sex, even if you are in love… Did you know that kissing will lead you to sex?" She went on non-stop.

I stared at her in shock, as she gave me her version of the birds and the bees. I let out a big heavy sigh and slumped on my bed, "can you change the subject, I don't want to talk about sex either, --- is not like I don't know already."

She gasped astounded, "you do?"

"Not the way you think." I answered quickly and continued, "Newsflash mom, there are plenty of other ways to learn about sex."

"Oh, yes sure," she sighed in relief and smiled.

"So, if this talk came about because of the new neighbor, don't worry ---I am not interested in him at all, or in anyone else for that matter," I got under the covers and fluffed my pillow.

"So, I'm guessing you are still a virgin?"

"Mom!" My eyes widened.

She chuckled, "Ok… ok, I'll stop."

"Mom, do you mind turning off the lights?"
She turned off the lights on her way out, "Goodnight honey."
"Goodnight mom."

CHAPTER 2

My mother dropped me off at the school on her way to see her doctor, and as soon as I entered the school, I saw Victor walking to his locker. I hid from him behind a group of kids, but I think he saw me. I saw him turned his head and stare in my direction. I quickly walked to my locker, I was so glad my locker was on the other end of the hallway from his, that way I wouldn't bump into him so often, but I still did. I saw him a few more times during the day, actually, it was more times than I wanted to, it seemed like he was on every turn or hallway I took. I did my best to avoid him by making up excuses, but the best way to escape his presence was when the popular girls would surround him. I just could not bring myself to talk to him, even if he was drop-dead gorgeous. I just did not feel like talking to him, today or ever. He gave me goose bumps all over, his presence made me jittery and I felt completely awkward around him.

At the end of the school day, I waited outside for my mother to pick me up.

Victor walked out of the school, "Hi again neighbor, do you need a ride?" He asked cheerfully when he saw me.

"It's Amber and no, thanks, ---I am waiting for my mom."

"Ok, I'll see you later Amber," he walked away.

I watched him as he strolled down to the silver Audi parked in the school parking lot and I saw him get in his car, but he did not leave.

I called my mom on her cell phone, but the call went straight to voice mail. Unable to reach her, I left her a message. Where is she? What is taking her so long? I said to myself as I watched the dark clouds gather in the sky above me. I continued to wait outside. I could feel the temperature dropping. I watched as the parking lot quickly emptied, a few cars were still there and one of those cars was Victor's silver car.

The dark foreboding clouds burst, and the rain began to pour.

"Great!" I said to myself as hundreds of raindrops landed on me. I shielded from the cold rain with my backpack but that did not do me any good, I was getting soaked anyways.

Victor pulled in front of the school, and parked his car and ran toward me with a black oversized umbrella, "Don't be stubborn let me take you home or at least get in the car, before you blow away," he said when a sudden gust of wind blew, almost knocking his umbrella out of his hands.

Filled with embarrassment, I stared at him hopelessly, by this time we were both getting drenched by the rain.

"Come on Amber, please," he insisted. "I promise I won't bite," he grinned and grabbed me by the arm, "come on."

I looked at my watch, "My mom probably got caught at work or something," I shivered.

He took my backpack and carried it, "it's ok, come on let's get in the car." He opened the passenger door and let me in. He closed the umbrella and got in the driver's side. "Isn't this better than getting wet?" He smiled and turned the heater up when he saw that I was shivering.

"Thank you," I said with my teeth chattering.

"Do you want to continue waiting for her or would you rather I take you home?"

"Can we wait here a little bit longer; if she is not here in five minutes then you can take me home," I said.

"Sure," he nodded.

I was overwhelmed with guilt and shame. I did not know what to say. His kindness had shut me up.

He did not talk much either which it made it even more awkward being inside his car. This was a time when silence was not golden.

I wished he at least had the radio on. I looked straight ahead, my gaze fixed on the pouring rain, but I could feel his eyes on me.

Five long minutes of torturing silence passed.

"Should we go?" He asked.

"Yes, I don't think she is coming," I said feeling distressed and ashamed.

He grinned, "You don't speak too much, do you?"

"No," I said timidly.

He pulled his car in front of my house.

I was surprised to see my mother's car in the driveway.

"Your mom is home, do you think she forgot about you?"

"Maybe," I answered while depressing thoughts crossed my mind. Probably something went wrong at the doctor, I thought. I feared the worst; my stomach twisted into a knot.

"Are you ok? You look upset."

I glanced at him, my eyes met his for a short moment, "I'm ok, ---thank you for bringing me home," I said humbly as I carefully studied his hazel eyes, and noticed that the green and golden brown colors swirled together making them look like marbles. His mesmerizing eyes swiftly drew me in. Suddenly, I found myself locked in a deep stare with him.

I finally broke the spell, and glanced out of the car window. I was afraid of what I was about to confront. "I should go. Thanks again," I opened the car door and ran up the porch steps and stood outside the front door with the keys in my hand; I then took a deep breath hoping for the best and waiting for the worst. I opened the door. "Mom, I'm home, —hello? —mom where are you?" I yelled and went to the kitchen to see if she was there, but the kitchen looked as impeccable as she had left it this morning. "Mom," I called again, and ran upstairs to her room. I found her lying on her bed.

She sat up when I entered her room. She wiped the tears from her face. Her eyes were gleaming and swollen from crying.

I ran to her and hugged her.

Her tears gave her away. I did not need words to know that something had gone wrong.

"Honey," she sobbed and wiped her nose with a crumbled tissue. "I'm so sorry I didn't pick you up, I came home straight from the doctor's office and loss track of time. Look at you, —you are soaking wet."

"Never mind that, what did the doctor say?"

She took a deep breath, "The cancer is back, honey," she sniffled and took a long pause, "and it's not good; it has spread to other parts of my body."

"Mom!" I felt my heart ripped into pieces. Unstoppable tears rolled down my face. My worst fear had turned into a reality. "Can it be treated?" I sobbed.

"Yes, I start treatment right away. But that is only going to prolong the inevitable."

"Mom, don't say that."

"I am just preparing you Amber, you're older now, and you need to know the truth, ---I won't last long."

I closed my eyes and squeezed them tight, the pain I felt was excruciating. I gulped, "How long do you think it will be? ---did the doctor say?" My voice cracked.

"Six months, maybe a year, if I am lucky."

I felt sick to my stomach, my legs felt like jelly, but I kept calm and my posture straight as best as I could.

"I am sorry I forgot to pick you up. —how did you get home?"

"Don't worry mom, the neighbor ---hmm Victor gave me a ride. Since it was raining I accepted his offer, I hope that was ok."

"Victor, huh?" She smiled, her red nose shined from crying so much. "Do you want me to get dinner ready?" She offered and brushed a strand of damped hair away from my face.

"No, mom, you should rest, ---I think we still have leftover lasagna from yesterday in the fridge; I'll warm it up."

"Ok, but change your clothes first, I don't want you to catch a pneumonia."

"Oh mom! ---as if," I forced myself to smile.

I saw her grab her jacket, and slowly put it on.

My mother was always so cheerful and full of energy. She was an attractive young woman with gorgeous golden brown hair passed her shoulders and beautiful green catlike eyes.

Sometimes I wished I had her looks, but not now, she had a wan expression on her face. It was heartrending to see her that way. Watching the cancer suck the life out of her. I could not stand the thought of losing her, but I had a plan for when that day came.

"Where are you going?" I asked.

"I forgot to drop off the prescriptions at the pharmacy."

I watched her lack of energy, she looked tired and a bit ashy, I was not going to let her get behind the wheels like that, "no, stay in bed, I told you to rest, I'll drop it off, give it here."

"Ok, but you are not taking the car," she told me.

"Ok, ok I'll walk. —where is the prescription?"

"In my purse, —but honey it's raining."

"Not anymore, I think finally the rain stopped," I said and I took the prescriptions from her purse and her credit card. I went to my room, put some dry clothes on and dry up my hair.

With my hair still a little damp, I grabbed my jacket and the multi-colored umbrella from the black medal holder by the door, and headed out the door to the pharmacy.

The rain had stopped, but menacing dark clouds lingered blocking the sunrays.

I saw Victor's car parked outside his house. The thought of asking him for a ride crossed my mind. I wondered if he would do me another favor. Probably not, I thought. I took a few steps down the sidewalk and stopped. I got gutsy, and turned around. What is the worst he can say or do? I thought to myself and grinned.

I walked to the front door of his house. I had my finger ready to push the doorbell, but immediately chickened out and lowered my hand and started to turn away. Then suddenly the door opened and a girl with short brownish red hair, on her way out bumped into me.

"Oh, I'm sorry, I didn't see you there," she said and caught me from falling.

I regained my balance, "Hi! Uhmm... is Victor here?"

"You must be Amber."

"Yes." My eyebrows furrowed, I wondered how she knew my name.

"Of course Victor is here, come on in," she said and called out for Victor. She stared at me and smiled. "I'm Emma, Victor's sister."

"Oh, it's nice to meet you, Emma," I smiled back.

Emma seemed pleasant and very charismatic, someone you would like to be friends with, but she kept checking me out from head to toe, and it made me feel ill at ease.

"He must be busy," I said and took a step towards the door ready to make my getaway.

"No, he is not, ---wait here I'll get him," she left the room and minutes later returned with Victor.

"Hey," he approached me. "Is everything ok?"

"Hmm... do you think you can give me a ride to the pharmacy?" I mumbled.

"Pardon me?" He leaned closer.

I repeated myself again, this time without mumbling and waited for his rejection.

He smiled. "Yeah sure, let me get my keys."

"You will?"

He looked bewildered, "Yes that's what I said, ---wait here I'll be right back."

His kindness made me feel guilty, I had been a total jerk to him at school today, just because of a stupid meaningless dream, and he was turning to be harmless.

"Is everything ok?" Emma asked.

"Yes, I have to get a prescription filled out for my mom."

"Oh, is she sick?"

"Yes."

Victor walked back into the living room, "let's go."

Emma walked with us outside, "bye, Amber," she said before getting in her car.

"Bye," I waved and smiled at Emma.

Victor opened the door for me.

"Your sister is very ---friendly and observant."

"I apologize if she stared at you," he put the keys in the ignition and started the car.

"That's alright, ---I was surprised she knew who I was."

"Well that was my fault, I talked about you earlier."

"Oh," I smiled and continued, "---thanks for giving me a ride. I didn't want to bother you, but it was sort of an emergency."

"You are not bothering me. I'm glad that you asked me," he grinned.

"I know how to drive, I just don't have my driver's permit yet... and you know how moms are," I giggled nervously.

"It's ok, you don't need to explain," he smiled and took his eyes off the road for few seconds to look at me, "do I make you feel uncomfortable?"

I giggled again, "Not really..." I cringed lower into the seat, yearning for the seat to swallow me.

He snickered and kept his eyes on the road without saying anything else.

I think he noticed how tense I was. I cleared my throat and said, "Victor, ---I know I have been a butthead to you, without having a good reason. I'm not rude all the time, you know. I can be nice too, I--- I just wanted to clear that up," I confessed and lowered my head.

He chuckled, "Is that some sort of an apology?"

"Uh-huh," I smiled sheepishly.

"You're not just cute, but funny too," he chuckled.

I sort of started to give him a flirty look, but immediately recognized what I was doing and masked my indiscretion with a serious look.

"Apology accepted," he smiled triumphantly and continued, "Is your mom sick? I heard you tell Emma the medicine was for your mom."

"Yes, she is very ill," I got misty eyes, but I held back the tears.

"Do you want to talk about it?"

I looked at him and bit my lips. I could not bring myself to confide in him and spill out all of my misery to a total stranger.

"Don't hide in your shell again, ---come on you were doing so well, you were talking, finally opening up a little, ---I even saw a convincing smile a couple of times," he grinned.

"I don't like talking to strangers."

"Oh I see, so is it common for you to ask strangers for a ride?"

"No. What I meant was that I didn't want to talk."

"Are you being rude again?"

"Oh no! Not at all."

He scoffed.

I saw the pharmacy up ahead and immediately smiled. Deep inside my twisting stomach, I felt as if, I was been rescued. "Uhm, can you pull in that shopping center, there is the pharmacy." I pointed it to him.

"Sure."

He parked right outside the pharmacy's entrance.

"Do you want to come with me?" I asked just to be polite.

"I sure do, I would be upset, if you didn't ask."

I caught myself giving him a flirty smile.

We walked in to the drugstore, all the way to the back to the pharmacist counter and I gave the prescription to the pharmacist.

"It will be ready in about thirty minutes to an hour," the pharmacist said.

"Ok," I said to the pharmacist and then turned to Victor, "you can leave me here. ---I'll find a way back home."

"I don't mind waiting," he shook his head.

"Are you sure?"

"Yes, I'm sure. I saw a Café next door; would you like to wait there? I'll get you a hot chocolate or coffee whichever you prefer," he smiled softly.

I gazed down to the white tiled floor, "Why are you being so nice to me?" I return my gaze back to him. My eyes were full of embarrassment and shame.

"I just want to talk some more and get to know you better, that way I won't be a stranger to you anymore, is that ok?" He gave me a wicked smile.

Of course, I could not contain myself and smiled back at him. I could not keep my eyes off him either. His facial features were so adorable, his smile enchanting, his eyes captivating and intriguing, and oh boy his mouth was scrumptious. I silently sighed with pleasure, "Sure let's go," I answered.

We went next door and walked to the counter to place an order.

He bought me a hot cocoa, but did not get himself any, which it seemed odd, since he is the one that suggested going there.

"Aren't you going to get one?" I asked.

"No, I'm good. I don't want the drink to get in the way of us talking," he grinned. "Is it ok if I ask you a few questions?"

We sat at a small wooden bistro table near the window. I could feel the cold coming through the glass.

This time I did not mind if we played the 20 questions game. I actually was enjoying being in his presence.

"About what?" I asked curiously.

"Tell me anything, what do you like to do, what type of music you listen to?" He asked.

I took a sip and wiped the whipped cream off my lips with the white paper napkin. "I don't go out much; I like to read a lot to keep my mind busy, ---and I enjoy all types of music."

"Do you have a boyfriend?"

His question caught me off guard.

"Uh —why?"

"Because... I don't want some jealous nut coming over here because I'm talking to his girlfriend." He looked around the café.

"Are you scared?" I smiled.

"No, it's his safety I'm worried about," he grinned and stared at me, "so, do you have one?"

I chuckled, "No. Do you have a girlfriend?"

"No."

"Liar," I said.

He gasped, "Why do you say that?"

"You have to have a girlfriend."

"Why?" He smiled mischievously.

"Hmm... because you're hot..." I said without thinking. "I mean that you drive a hot, I mean nice car." I giggled, "I know you must have lots of girls after you." I could feel the blood rushing to my face. I held my breath and hoped that he did not hear me say that he was hot.

He leaned back on the chair, "So, you find me hot, huh?" He smiled conceitedly.

I could feel my face had turned hot red. I covered my beet red face with both hands, and did not answer him.

He laughed. "I'm not interested in those girls; there is only one that I'm very interested in. She is the love of my life, she's my soul mate."

"Oh!" I said trying not to sound so disappointed, then looked down at my cup and slowly rubbed my finger around the rim and wondered who she was, "---is she here in town or did you leave her behind where ever you came from?" I asked and took another sip of the hot cocoa. I looked back at him as I waited for his answer.

I caught him staring at me deeply, in a very unusual way. Just like someone before going for the first kiss, but I was sure that could not be it.

The long staring contest made me feel self-conscious, "do I have something on my face?" I instantly cleaned my mouth with the napkin.

"No, I was admiring you. You are very beautiful Amber," he continued to stare.

My heart started to beat faster; I felt my face blush again, I know I must have looked like a chameleon turning different shades of red. I did not know what to say, but even with my tongue-tied, I was able to blabber foolishly, "your sister is very beautiful too."

He chuckled and shook his head, "I guess so, but that's her husband business not mine."

"She is married?"

"Yes, his name is Max. I don't think you have met him yet. He's a really nice guy," he commented.

"But she looks so young," I said amazed.

He laughed, "she is way older than you think."

"Huh… I guess she just looks young then."

"You've got that one right," he smiled. He stared at the multicolored friendship bracelet I was wearing and reached to see it. His hand accidentally touched mine; the fingertips of his fingers were very cold.

I quickly moved my hand away. "Your fingers are cold," I smiled nervously and rubbed my hands together to warm them.

"Sorry, I just wanted to see your bracelet," he said with a sense of guilt and looked down at his hands.

I had made him feel self-conscious. I took off my bracelet and showed it to him. He carefully returned it back to me, trying to avoid touching my skin.

"That's alright. My hands are always cold too, especially in this type of weather." I smiled at him trying to cheer him up.

"Can I ask you something?"

"Sure." I replied.

"Are you the only girl down our street named after a precious stone?" He asked with a straight face.

I chuckled, "What?"

"Is there any other girl down the street from us with a name like Ruby or Esmeralda?" His face was expressionless.

"You're joking right?" I asked incredulously and raised my left eyebrow slightly.

"No, I'm not," he answered in a serious tone.

It was impossible for me to hold in the laugh, "Uh-uh you're pulling my leg," I said laughing.

"No. Can you just please answer me."

I stopped laughing when I saw that he seemed a little ticked off, "ok," I said with skepticism and gazed at him trying to keep myself from not laughing, "Why? ---do you collect them?"

"No," he answered in a dry tone. He did not seem amused.

I cleared my throat, "Wow, ---you are dead serious. That is the weirdest question, I've ever been asked," I was stunned.

"I'm glad I'm making you laugh. Now, can you answer me?"

I chuckled, "Well sure, there was an old lady named Opal but she passed away."

"Really?" He looked surprised.

I giggled, "No silly, I'm kidding."

He scoffed and tapped the table with his fingers impatiently.

I then commented with a controlled smile, "Ok, the only girls down our streets are Chloe, Monica and Ashley. I think you know them already, I saw you talking to them during lunch."

"Oh those girls ---they're not my type."

I grinned when I heard him say that. I finally met a boy that was not after those floozies.

"So, you are the only one then?" He pursued with the odd question.

"I'm positive, ---but seriously now, why do you ask?" I inquired about this weird obsession with jewels' name.

"Just making conversation, that's all," he said in a casual tone and serious face.

"But that was so... random and super weird," I said with mock astonishment. "---if you want to make conversation why don't you ask about the weather or something like that, ---you know what's your sign? Get it?"

"But that is cheesy."

I scoffed "Whatever ---better cheesy than weird," I muttered and rolled my eyes.

"Are you finished?" He asked.

"No, I still have a little more, do you want some?" I said feeling slightly angered.

"No, I'm ok, thank you," he answered.

I was still a bit mad at him for taking me for a fool, but I had to be nice, he was my ride home, anyways he had his soul mate, she can deal with his weirdness. Then I remembered he never answered me, I really wanted to know who she was. I glanced at him, I saw that he was smiling, "you never answered me the question about the girl you are interested in."

"I will tell you about her some other time."

"Why not now?" I insisted. I was very intrigued to find out who was the love of his life.

"Because she lives here in town," he answered.

"But you said you didn't know anyone here."

"I see you were paying attention," he grinned.

"So, you're lying again," I accused.

"I haven't lied," he smiled.

I felt deceived by him, what is up with him? I wondered why he was playing games. All this time he acted as if he did not know a soul in this town, but why should I care? I thought to myself.

We continued talking.

He asked me why my mother had named me Amber.

I told him that when I was born I had honey colored eyes, so my mother named me after the stone. I was either going to be Amber or Honey. I try to get some information about his family but he avoided all those questions and after a while, I just gave up.

Thirty minutes have passed. We went to pick up the prescriptions from the pharmacy next door.

After that, we walked back to the car and he held the door open for me.

He was weird but he was a gentleman.

Little by little, he had gained my confidence. I don't know how he did it, but I felt more at ease in his presence, so I divulged to him what I painfully carried inside my heart. "My mom has terminal cancer, she probably won't live long," I said to him.

"I'm sorry, Amber."

"She is all I have," My voice cracked, I could not hold the tears back.

He put the car back to parking and stopped the engine. He moved closer and hugged me.

My face buried on his chest, tears rolled down my cheeks.

"Please don't cry," he said softly and gently touched my face with his cold hand and wiped my tears away.

His body got rigid and he pulled me closer.

"Are you ok?" I asked sobbing. His chest felt like a brick

wall.

"Yes. I just don't want to see you cry, it hurts me too," he held me in his arms, and pressed me against his stiff chest.

"Why? ---you don't know me, we just met," I said and tried to look up at his face, but he quickly pushed my head back down to his chest.

"I know you better than you think." He whispered in my ear.

I felt unease being so close to him, so I started to wiggle my way out of his arms. Then I faintly heard him say something else, which it sounded like, *'don't fight it'* but I did not know what he meant by it.

"Hmm did you say something?" I asked.

"No," he answered softly.

Then a strange sensation overwhelmed me, and I suddenly stopped struggling to get away and started enjoying every second he held me in his arms.

The smell of his cologne was appealing and seductive.

For an instant I had gone to heaven, but then reality hit me, I was letting a total stranger hold me, my guts were telling me to be careful but deep inside my heart something beautiful was flourishing. I finally realized the meaning of this forbidden feeling I was finding hard to ignore, —I desired Victor. I closed my eyes and drifted away in his arms, wanting that moment to last forever.

He lifted my chin, and our eyes met again.

He took a deep breath, "I should take you home now. I don't want your mom to worry."

I slowly moved back to my seat, "Are you ok?" I asked again and gave him an inquisitive look.

"Yes, just that... I got a little emotional and I didn't want you to see me."

He was adorable and sexy but then I again, I could be wrong, his reaction seemed odd and overly sensitive, I thought and smiled, "it's ok if you are sensitive," I said sympathetically.

"But I am not like that, it's just that..." He seemed to be irritated.

Oops! I had offended him. I think he thought I was calling him gay. It was not exactly a foot in the mouth type of moment, but I had managed to embarrass myself quite nicely. I responded rather quickly and tried to smooth things, "I didn't mean it in a derogative way."

He grinned understanding that was not what I tried to say. "I know," he paused for a moment before continuing, "where is your dad in all of this?"

"He left us when I was a month old, I never met him. A few years back I learned that he died. I have no other family, but my mom."

"Sorry."

"It's ok, it's not like I knew him." I pursed my lips slightly; I did not like to talk about my loser dad. "Can we go now? ---I need to take these to her."

When he started the car again, I saw he had a tissue crumbled on his other hand; there was some blood in it, I wondered if he had cut himself or if he had a nosebleed.

"What happened? Did you cut yourself?"

"No," he answered convincingly.

I pointed at his hand with the crumbled tissue.

"Oh, this?" He grinned, "It's nothing," he rolled down the window and quickly tossed it outside before driving away. "Amber, can you promise me something?"

"It depends, what is it?"

We came to a stop at the red light.

He turned to me and said kindly, "If you ever need anything please come and get me, don't be scare to ask me, I won't turn you down. I would like to be there for you and your mom, if you let me. Is that ok? Can you promise me that?" He smiled at me.

I tilted my head to the side, his kindness got to me again, "Sure---but why are you being so nice to me?"

He glanced at me, "Do I have to have a reason?"

"Hmm... no, not really," I pouted and looked out of the window.

Victor pulled into our driveway. "Let me go in with you," he offered.

"No! You don't have to, really." I was afraid my mom would see us, "thanks for everything." I said with a fond smile. After a short moment of reflection, I continued, "You are not so bad after all, a little strange but not bad," I grinned.

"I'm going to take that as a compliment," he winked.

"Bye, Victor."

"Amber, wait!" He took my hand.

His hand was still clammy and cold, but this time I let him hold it.

"Can I take you to school tomorrow--- well that is if your mom is not able to, of course."

"Uh... maybe, if she says is ok," I answered, even though I knew that my mom would not approve.

"I'll stop in the morning to see if you need a ride."

"Sure, —thank you again Victor."

"Have a good night, Amber."

His eyes captivated my gaze and his mesmerizing eyes were drawing me in once more.

He let go of my hand and smiled mischievously.

I blushed and said, "you too," as I grinned from ear to ear. I had just experience a short moment of pure bliss in this horrible miserable day.

I quickly went up the porch steps. I felt the butterflies in my stomach slowly calming down before I opened the front door. I took the medicines to my mother and stayed with her talking for a couple of hours until she fell asleep.

The doorbell rang.

The first person that came to my mind was Victor. I felt my heart leap. I dropped the magazine I was reading on the floor and I ran excitedly downstairs to open the door.

I was disillusioned when I saw who it was.

My least favorite person, Chloe was at the door. She had sandy blond hair, somewhat pretty, and very stuck-up.

"Hi Amber, can I talk to you for a minute."

Her visit was unusual and unwanted, but I greeted her anyways, "Sure, what is it Chloe?"

"Just a warning, you shouldn't follow Victor like an abandoned puppy. You're making a fool out of yourself. I don't think he is into little girls," she said condescending.

She caught me off guard but I answered wittily, "he may not be, but he is not interested in your type either," I could feel my blood boiling already.

"Maybe because I am not throwing myself at him the way you are, but just wait, I'm having a party next weekend and he is coming, you'll see how interested in me he is after that," she tossed her hair, "but then again, freshmen are not invited, so you won't be able to see him drooling after me."

"For your information I'm not a freshman and who cares about your stupid party," the sight of her alone made me sick, I felt a little puke come up my throat.

"Well whatever. Just stop offering yourself to him; he is way out of your league," she said with a smug.

"I'm not offering myself to him, you dimwit." I refrained myself from calling her something else.

"Oh no? I saw you and him in his car; you were all over him, kissing him."

"I didn't kiss him," I responded.

"Sure you didn't."

I wanted to rip her sandy blond hair off her scalp, "go to hell," I said enraged.

"Aww is somebody getting upset?"

I smirked, "No, I'm just getting sick of hearing your voice." I squeezed the door handle wishing that it were her skinny neck. "Just leave and don't come to my house ever again," I said with my teeth clenched.

"Oh I won't, — it smells like trash in here."

"Then go breathe somewhere else, bitch!" I slammed the door on her face.

"Argh!! I can't stand her." I yelled and stumped back upstairs. I walked by my mother's room and sighed in relief when I saw that she had slept through the ruckus and especially that she did not hear me curse.

CHAPTER 3

It had only been a week since I met Victor, but somehow to me it seemed longer. Every morning I would wake up looking forward to seeing and talking to him on the hallway at school. And then after school when he would stop by my house to check on me and my mom, at least that's the excuse he would give me for coming over. The front porch turned out to be our hang out place.

Victor was very caring, protective and lamentably very respectful to me. I wished he would hug me the way he did that first time he unlocked this desire in me, but I could not let him know I had a crush on him.

Although sometimes I thought he was interested in me too, just by the way he looked at me. The desire in his eyes was impossible to ignore. I just thought that he was not acting on his feelings because he was a few years older than I was or maybe it was because of that girl he said he was in love with.

I sighed, and wished I could be so lucky to be that girl. I checked myself in the mirror and went to my mother's room and I stood by the open door. I was surprised to see her still under the covers.

She sat up when she saw me there, "hi honey, come in," she said sluggishly.

BUTTERFLY KISSES

I noticed the state she was in, "you can't take me to school today, can you?" I said bleakly.

"No sweetie, do you think you can catch a ride with Victor?"

"Yes sure, I'll ask him, —I just hope he still there."

"Tell him I'll gladly pay for his gas, and don't forget to thank him for me."

"Sure mom. Are you going to be ok all alone?"

"I should be. The doctor is supposed to call this morning with the test results, after that if he doesn't need me to go see him, I'll head on to the office."

"Text me, if you need me, I'll have the cell phone on vibrate," I looked at the time on my watch. I was late I had ten minutes to get to school.

I kissed her on the forehead and rushed downstairs, hoping that Victor had not left yet, but when I opened the door, Victor was waiting for me.

He was leaning against one of the post on the porch, "Ready?"

"Yes, but how did you know?"

"Your mom called me earlier and asked me if I could to take you, because she wasn't feeling well."

"She has your number?"

"Yes, ---are you jealous?" He grinned mischievously.

I snickered, "No."

"Get in, we are late," he opened the door. "Where are your books?"

"Oh I don't need them today, we have a field trip."

"Oh really, ---where are you going?" He asked.

"Our biology class is going to the Arboretum."

"Can I go?"

"No, it's only for the tenth graders."

"Don't you need a chaperone? I can meet you there," he grinned.

"No, thanks. You'll just get me in trouble with the teacher, and I'll probably spend a Saturday in d-hall because of you."

That reminded me that Chloe's party was coming up, I was curious to know if he was going or not, so I asked him. Surprisingly, he told me he was not sure yet, and asked me if I wanted to go with him, but I had to decline since I was officially uninvited by the snob princess herself.

Victor seemed to be bothered by the fact that Chloe had been rude to me, but I told him that I did not care, that it was not a big deal to me because I hated her too; and that sort of calmed him down because his demeanor suddenly changed, —I saw him grin.

He pulled in the school's parking lot. He got out and opened the door for me before I even had the chance to reach for the latch.

"Thank you," I said amazed by his swiftness.

"You're welcome."

"Amber!" Brad shouted from across the parking lot.

I turned and saw Brad standing by the school bus.

Brad's husky built and shaggy black hair, were somewhat intimidating.

I smiled and waved.

Victor turned around, "Who is that?"

"That's Brad he is in my biology class."

"Huh. Is he your boyfriend?" He asked glancing back at Brad.

"No, I told you I don't have a boyfriend," I shut the car door.

"I don't like him," he said bluntly and gave Brad a hateful look.

"Victor!" I reproached.

"I'm being honest," he replied.

"He is harmless; he just likes to dress that way…" I glanced at Brad, "He is into that rocker gothic look, ---it's kind of his thing, you know."

"No, I don't know," Victor's expression was grim and threatening.

I shook my head and let out a loud sigh.

Victor had his awkward moments, but this time it was different. I could not understand his bizarre behavior toward Brad, unless--- he was jealous, I thought and grinned. "I have to go, they are loading the bus. Thanks for the ride."

"Don't forget I'm taking you home."

"I won't, – just don't leave without me." I walked toward the bus.

Brad waited for me and hurried in behind me, when I climbed up the bus' steps.

I sat next to Carly; Brad sat on the seat in front of us and turned around to talk to us. I looked out the window and Victor was still standing by his car, with a very preoccupied look on his face, and as soon as the bus driver closed the doors, Victor got in his car and left. I could not believe my eyes, the fact that he was skipping school made me chuckle inside. I only hoped he would remember to come back to pick me up.

The noise inside the bus seemed to intensify; everyone seemed to be talking at the same time. However, the sound of the bus engine idling made some of them stop and get in their seats, and we left the school grounds.

Carly took off her knitted purple hat, she then messed her bangs with her fingers. "Who was that?" Carly asked in a loud tone.

"That's Victor, my neighbor," I answered, and wondered where he went.

"I have seen him talking to you before on the hallway, ---he is cute," Carly commented.

"Isn't he?" I raised my brows and grinned.

"He is too old for you," Brad said judgmental.

"Oh shut up! She is just saying he is cute," Carly rolled her blue eyes.

"I like your new look," I complimented her.

"Thanks, I got rid of my old glasses, now I just need to get used to these contacts," she blinked a few times battering her eyelashes.

"You look very pretty, doesn't she, Brad?" I said.

Brad grunted and then he put his headphones on without answering me, and rudely turned his back on us.

"Brad, I am talking to you." I flicked him with my finger on the back of his head but he did not turn, "what's his problem?" I asked Carly.

"Don't mind him, he just acting stupid. I think he is jealous of your new friend."

I scoffed.

Finally, after the bumpy ride on the bus, we arrived at the Arboretum.

At the visitor's center, our class watched a short instructional film. Then Mr. Morris, our teacher handed each one of us a map and an information sheet with the names of plants and trees, then Mr. Morris took us out to our nature trail walk.

We followed the teacher through the trails.

Carly slowed down when she noticed two squirrels playing chase. "Look Amber over there, isn't that adorable," she said with a big smile.

"Aw, how cute."

We stopped to watch the squirrels play, but then the squirrels stopped abruptly as if they had sensed danger, and immediately ran away.

"Huh, that was weird, they seemed scared," Carly frowned.

"I think they were too busy playing and finally saw us."

"Yeah maybe," she giggled.

I felt like someone was watching me and I turned around. Victor was standing in the distance, down the path we had already walked through.

"Hey isn't that your friend?" Carly noticed him too.

"Yes. Please don't say anything--- I'll catch up."

"Where are you going?" She grabbed my arm.

"I'm just going to talk to him, ---it's ok."

"Are you sure you're going to be ok?" Carly asked concerned.

"Yes, ---I'll be just a moment. They won't even know I'm gone, and if they ask just say that I had to go back to use the ladies room."

"Ok, but be careful," Carly scurried down the trail.

Victor walked toward me.

"Why are you following me?" I whispered.

"I wanted to make sure you were ok," he spoke in a subdue manner.

"And why wouldn't I be?"

He shrugged, "Just a bad feeling."

"So, that's your reason for skipping school?"

"Who cares if I miss school? I wanted to come with you, I told you."

"Yeah, and I also told you that if my teacher sees you here, I'm going to get in trouble." I said with a pinched expression on my face.

"Then let's go," he suggested and pulled me away from the trail.

Although the thought of going with him was provocative, I

promptly stopped walking and stubbornly stood still, "No! Are you crazy?" I sighed and shook my head, "please go, I'll be fine, I promise not to trip over a root." I snickered

He did not seem to care for my humor. "Where is your friend Brad?"

"I don't know Victor, somewhere up ahead, why?"

"I really don't like him," he said irritably.

"Oh, please! Victor, just go!"

He turned away just to spin right back, his arms on his side, his open hands turned fist, which he opened and closed in anger, "I don't want you talking to him."

I flinched, "but he is a friend —just like we are."

"It's different for us..." He said in a stern voice and suddenly stopped when something got his attention.

"Amber!" I heard my teacher call my name in the distance.

My eyes widened, I was scared that the teacher would catch me with him. "Go!"

"I'll go, but I'll be following you," he said.

"No!"

"Don't worry they won't see me," he assured.

"Amber." The teacher called my name again, but this time he sounded closer.

I panicked and glanced back to where Victor was standing, but he was already gone. I spun around searching for him, but I could not see him. Then suddenly portions of the dream played back in my head, I remembered seeing Victor in a field just like this one, the only difference was that he was chasing me. The thought of it sent chills down my spine. "I'm coming Mr. Morris," I shouted and got back on the trail.

"Amber, I told you to stay together with the class," Mr. Morris said when he saw me.

"Yes, but I needed to use the restroom."

"Hmm... next time ask me first. ---hurry up we need to catch up with the group, I don't want to lose another student."

The rest of the day, I could feel someone watching me, it was an eerie feeling, then I thought of Victor, but it could not have been him, I think I would had seen him.

We loaded the bus and headed back to school. During the drive back, I felt jumpy, I could not understand why. I kept checking my watch. I guess I just wanted to see him.

Then the bus drove around the parking lot and came to a stop in front of the school. I exited the bus, and I noticed Victor's silver Audi in the parking lot, but he was not around.

"Is your mom coming for you?" Carly asked.

"No, she is busy today."

"Do you need a ride? My dad is coming for me," Carly offered.

"Uhm no thanks, I think I have a ride," I said hoping that Victor was inside the school, I turned around to take a quick look where his car was and saw that Victor was now standing there. I smiled but I tried not to show my excitement, "Victor is waiting for me."

"Oh brother, what's wrong with that dude?" Brad sneaked behind us and put his arms around us. "Is he always following you?" Brad asked.

I immediately noticed Victor's livid expression.

"Look at him he think he can intimidate me," Brad said with a smug.

"Shut up Brad, leave him alone," Carly said.

"Yeah don't mess with him he'll kick your butt," I chuckled.

"I would pay to see that," Carly laughed.

We both took Brad's arms off from us. We were still mad at him for behaving like an obnoxious idiot earlier.

"I have to go, he is waiting. Uhm Carly, are you going to Chloe's party?" I asked.

"Hell no! That snob didn't invite me, ---but I would love to crash it just to piss her off," she snickered.

"Yeah, me too," I laughed.

"Amber, are you ready?" I heard Victor say.

I turned and he was standing right behind me, "Yes, let's go."

Carly cleared her throat, "Hi I'm Carly," she introduced herself.

"Nice to meet you Carly, I'm Victor," he smiled pleasantly.

"Yeah I know," Carly giggled.

"And you are Bradley," Victor demeanor was unfriendly.

"It's Brad... not Bradley," Brad said with arrogance.

Victor snickered, "whatever," he rolled his eyes and turned to Carly, intentionally ignoring Brad. "Take care Carly."

Carly smiled, "Yes, you too."

"Let's go Amber." Victor lightly touched my back sending an electric current through my body.

"Bye Carly —bye Brad."

I saw Brad pouting angrily and he did not reply to me.

"Later girl." Carly answered.

Victor held the car door open as I sat down inside the car.

"That wasn't nice; you didn't have to be rude to Brad," I gave him a judgmental look.

He slammed shut the passenger door and walked around and got behind the wheel. "Why do you care, if I was rude to him or not, he is not your boyfriend?"

"No, but I have known him since we were in fifth grade."

"Do you like him?"

"No!" I answered firmly and looked at him. "He is just a friend."

His eyes met mine. His gaze was piercing as if trying to read my thoughts.

I started to feel that ardent desire again. I remembered the dream; I did not know what to believe anymore. The only thing I was sure of was that I really liked him. I closed my eyes and took a deep breath to cool down the fire inside me, "did you stay at the Arboretum?"

"Why?"

"You kind a disappeared on me after we talked and you said you were going to follow me."

"I left," he said in a dry tone.

"Oh," I said disappointed. I guess my intuition of someone following me had been wrong, I thought.

When we got home, he parked his car in his driveway.

I stared at the big house, then I turned around to look at my house and I noticed my mother was not home.

"Amber," Victor held my hand. He had not done this since that blissful first day.

I smiled and gazed at him. I had butterflies dancing in my stomach, "Yes, Victor."

"I need to be honest with you, ---because I want the same from you in return."

"What is it?" I felt my stomach drop afraid of what he was

about to tell me.

"I did follow you, I'm sorry," he lowered his eyes and returned his gaze to me, "I didn't tell you earlier because I didn't want you to get mad at me, sorry. —I just needed to make sure nothing happened to you."

I rested my head on the seat and I huffed. What made him think I was not going to get mad at him now, I thought. But because I valued our friendship, I was willing to forgive his white lie. I understood his reason for lying but I am not sure I understood his concerns. "What did you think was going to happen to me? It was a harmless field trip, —it wasn't like I was jumping out of a plane or something."

"It wasn't that," he paused, "it's just that, I don't trust your friend Brad, he is giving me some bad vibes."

"Do you trust me?"

"Yes I do," he gently touched my face with the back of his cold fingers.

I closed my eyes, "Victor, don't."

He leaned forward and whispered in my ears, "My precious Amber."

I felt his lips softly touch my ear. The same feeling of bliss sneaked back on me. I was feeling euphoric. My heart was going to leap out of my chest. I wanted to kiss him so bad, but I resisted the urge and opened my eyes, "Victor, I have to go." I reached to open the door.

"Can I visit you later? I have something for you."

"Hmm, I don't know. People are starting to talk."

"Who Brad?"

"No, Chloe."

"So what?"

"You don't know her very well; she'll start rumors about me."

"Did she say something to you?"

I told him what she had said to me that day she saw us outside the pharmacy and that seemed to tick him off again. He was not too happy after that, I could see his neck and shoulders getting tense.

I secretly smiled inside, I could sense that he was beginning not to like her and I could not blame him.

He narrowed his eyes and gave me a dark look, "So you are

going to stop seeing me because of what she said?"

My mind froze then it started churning again. I wished he would just come out and tell me that he was interested in me. But it just seemed like he was dropping hints, "no, I didn't say that. It's just that we shouldn't hang around so much, remember I'm younger than you," I deliberately said that and I waited to see what he would say. I gazed at him with excitement. I wanted him to spill out his guts and tell me once and for all what he felt for me.

"What does age have to do with us being friends?"

I felt like I had just shot myself in the foot. Friends? I said to myself and looked away. I thought the age difference was the factor in him not coming forward with his true feelings. I was really hoping he would say that he loved me, but no, we are just friends. I shook my head, "Nothing." I said disillusioned.

"Ok then." he smiled and grabbed my hand again and held it.

I was getting a whiplash from all his mixed signals, "but people are going to think there is something more between us, when there isn't, —some might even call you a pervert." I persisted hoping that he would withdraw his friend remark.

He snickered, "I don't care what they think, or say, —I just know what I…" He stopped himself mid-sentence.

"You know what?"

"Forget it," he looked away and stared forward at his house.

Just freaking say it, I shouted inside my head, I could feel my face turning red, "what you want? Is that what you were going to say?"

He hit the steering wheel with his hand, "yes," he snapped, "what I want, ok. What is mine, and no one is going to stand in my way," he said frustrated and stared at me.

"Are you saying that you want me?"

He bit his lips, he seemed to be hiding something, and he was not willing to divulge it to me, "is not what you think."

I felt my stomach twist with acid; it was like being in a rollercoaster ride. "Arrgh! I have to go Victor. Thanks for bringing me home," I stormed out of the car and went home.

I was so mad at him, one minute I am his friend and the next he wants me. I grabbed a magazine and aggressively flipped through the pages as I waited at home for my mother to get home from work. Then I went upstairs and changed clothes. Victor's words repeated in my head, he wants me, but not the way I think. I then concluded that maybe my dream was not so far off. Maybe he said he wants me is because he is after me.

I heard my stomach rumbling. I walked down to the kitchen to fix dinner. I put on the headset of my iPod and listened to music while I cooked. A Taylor Swift song started to play, I grabbed a spoon and used it as a microphone while I danced silly to the tune. When I twirled, I saw Victor leaning against the entrance to the kitchen watching me, enjoying the show.

"Ahh!" I ripped the headphones from my ears.

Victor laughed, and started to clap. "Impressive, remind me never to take you out dancing."

I blushed ashamed, "Shut up... what are you doing here? How did you come in?" I asked him.

"You left the front door unlocked," he smiled.

"So you just walk in?"

"No. You did not hear me knock. I brought you something... here," he handed me a paper bag.

"What is it?"

"A peace offering, open it."

I opened the bag, "It's a book, cool 'Romeo and Juliet' ---a classic. What makes you think I haven't read it yet, huh?"

"Just a wild guess."

I smiled. I had forgotten how mad I was at him earlier.

"Have you read it?"

"No, but I know the story," I glanced back at him. "Thank you. My mom was supposed to take me to the library to get a book, but she hasn't been able to."

"Well now you have something to read."

I smiled, "yes."

We stared into each other's eyes without saying a word.

The phone rang and startled us.

I went to answer it. The call was from my mother's office to inform me that she was in the hospital. I slowly hanged up the phone fearing the worst.

"What is it?" he put his hands on my shoulder.

I turned to face him, "My mom, she is in the hospital, please take me," I said as I came out of the frightened haze.

"Sure, let me get my keys," he headed to the front door.

"I'll meet you outside," I turned off the stove and grabbed the house keys and my jacket from the coat rack and proceeded to the door.

Victor was already standing outside waiting for me.

"Wow, you sure are fast."

He grinned and helped me put my jacket on. Victor speeded down the streets all the way to the hospital.

When we got to the emergency room, my mother was waiting for the discharge papers.

"What happened?" I asked her.

"Some idiot ran a light and hit us."

"Us? Who else was in the car?"

"Trisha."

"Oh, is she ok?" I asked.

"Yes, she didn't have a scratch. They only kept me because I had a nose bleed, but those are from the medicines I'm taking."

"So how bad is the damage to our car?"

"Oh no, our car is fine. I was in Trisha's car. She was driving. My car is parked at the office."

"Oh! I was hoping it was really damaged and we could get a new one," I grinned.

"Amber," my mother rebuked.

Victor smiled, "Mrs. Ross, do you want us to go get your car?"

"That's very nice of you Victor, but I don't let Amber drive yet."

"I didn't mean Amber. —I thought I could ask my brother in law or my dad to go with me."

My mother glanced at me, "Sure, if you don't mind," she said and turned her eyes back to him.

I looked at Victor. I could not take my beaming eyes off him.

"It's my pleasure," he smiled and shifted his eyes to me.

I smiled back a little flirty, but then I remembered we were not alone and I quickly shifted my glance toward my mother, who was looking at us carefully and shrewdly.

Victor took us home from the hospital after my mom signed all the papers.

I unlocked the front door, and entered the house.

"That poor boy is crazy about you," she said as she shut the door behind her. "What are your feelings for him? Are you leading him on?"

"No, mom... he is just a friend."

"A friend, huh? Every time I turn he is with you or helping you," she picked up the book from the kitchen table, "did you get this?" she raised her eyebrow.

"No."

"Let me guess Victor gave it to you?"

"Yeah ---but he is just trying to be nice. He knows I like to read."

"I'm sure he does," she put the book down on the table, "has he tried anything with you?"

"No, Mom. He is not like that, he is very respectful," I defended him.

"Honey, you know I like Victor but at that age ---boys are only thinking about one thing and that is sex," she shook her head.

I interrupted. "He is not that way mom, really."

"Don't be naïve, they all are, especially at his age... and don't forget you are only fifteen," she scoffed.

"I'm almost sixteen--- next week is my birthday in case you forgot," I raised my voice.

My mother and I argued. I could not understand her behavior I thought she liked Victor. I thought she wanted me to talk to him.

"Don't get me wrong, I do like Victor. He is a nice kid and I appreciate all his help taking you to school when I can't".

I could not understand her reasoning, "so what's the problem, mom."

She had an anguished expression, "I saw how you looked at him earlier, you can't fool me, and he certainly has feelings for you." She grabbed me by the shoulders and looked straight at me, "sweetie, under other circumstances I think he would have been a great match for you but you are still too young and the more time you spend alone with him, the more he is going to expect out of you."

I tried everything hoping she would reason with me, but I could not get her to understand that Victor was different, that he respected me. That all he wanted was to protect me.

Then the truth came out, the main reason she was so upset, she told me that the old woman next door had been gossiping about Victor and I, but mainly she was spreading rumors about me being promiscuous and doing other things. The news really shocked me. I was almost in tears.

"Do you think I like hearing things about you? So try not to hang with Victor anymore, at least until all the gossiping dies down, ok?"

I glanced down embarrassed, "but mom I am not doing anything."

"Baby, I am not going to be around for much longer to take care of you or to defend you from that old hag next door."

The thought of her leaving me made me upset. She was leaving me all alone and her only regret was what people would say about me. I got angry; my emotions were all mixed up. I raised my voice, "I can take care of myself I'm not nine years old, mom. I can tell that old lady where she can go," I had angry tears rolling down my face.

"Honey, I am just looking out for you future, can't you see that?"

"Then trust me," I snapped.

"How can I, when you spend so much time alone with Victor? I don't know what you two are doing when I am not around."

I felt resentment against my mother, "don't worry mom, I'm not following your footsteps, I won't make the same mistake you did by getting pregnant at sixteen and having an unwanted baby like you did."

My mother raised her hand and slapped me.

I felt my left cheek burning. I saw the disappointment in her eyes.

"Go to your room!" She shouted.

My eyes clouded with tears. I ran upstairs to my room and locked the door behind. I leaned against the door and started to cry, I was feeling remorseful and guilty for offending her but it was already too late, I could not take it back.

Later that evening, I saw Victor and his dad drop my mother's car. I saw him walking back to his house, but he did not turn around. I wondered if he knew I was standing by the window.

I could not sleep at all that night, I thought of sneaking out of the house to go see him. I peeked out of the window to see if they were up, but the lights in his house were off.

I went back to bed, I flipped and turned trying to get

comfortable, but still could not fall asleep; all I could think about was Victor. I was really falling for him, what I was feeling was more than a teenage crush. My mother was right I could not be trusted alone with Victor, not when I feel this way for him.

It was past midnight, I got up to use the restroom. On my way back to the bed, I peeked out of the window again, I then saw Victor, Emma and Mrs. Cromwell walking back to their house; it seemed like they had gone for a midnight stroll. This was not the first time I had seen one of them come home late from a walk, but never Victor. I was consumed with curiosity about their midnight escapades. I wanted to know what they were up to and I was determined to find out.

CHAPTER 4

After a restless night, I opened my eyes. I could still use a few more minutes of sleep, but the smell of freshly baked blueberry muffins was enough to get me up off the bed. I took a shower and went downstairs. I needed to apologize to my mother.

She was in the kitchen, placing the basket full of muffins on the table.

"Good morning mom," I gave her a kiss on the cheek.

"Good morning sleepy head. Do you want milk or juice?"

My mother was pouring herself some coffee on a cup. The aroma of the freshly brewed coffee made my mouth water besides I needed some caffeine to wake me up, so I asked for coffee instead.

She grinned and got another cup from the cupboard.

I looked at her while she poured the steaming coffee in a cup. "Mom, about last night, I'm…"

She cut in, "Shh! ---I am the one that is sorry. I know you better; I should trust you more, especially if you are telling me nothing is going on between you two. I just shouldn't have talked to you that way, and I definitely shouldn't have hit you, are you ok?"

"Yes, and I am sorry mom, I was out of line."

"Ok, we are both sorry," she chuckled. "How about a muffin?" She offered.

"Just one?" I said kidding.

She laughed, "you can have some more." She paused to think, and then she continued, "Amber I had a talk with Victor last night."

"Mom let's not talk about that, please," I begged.

"He is a good kid, and his family they are great, they brought him up good. I shouldn't worry about him, ---or you."

I sighed in relief, but still I could not believe what I was hearing. I wondered what he told her to bring this sudden change; maybe he finally said he loved me. I daydreamed for a short minute then I asked with enthusiasm, "What did he say?"

"Well, he wants the best for you, the same way I do."

I raised my eyebrows, "so is it ok if I continue to talk to him?" I bit my lips.

"Yes, of course. As a matter of fact he has invited us to Chez Vous, the French restaurant downtown."

"He did? I smiled. I was elated our first date, I was so happy I did not care that my mother was invited too, "when?"

"Tonight," she replied.

"Just us three?"

"I think he is bringing his mom and dad."

"Oh!" I said surprised. A feel of victory overwhelmed me, not only tonight was Chloe's party, which meant Victor was not going, but he wanted our parents to get to know each other, maybe someday, he will admit he loves me, I thought and grinned.

"What is it sweetheart?" My mother noticed my excitement.

"Nothing… these muffins are really good," I smiled and nodded my head.

Later in the day I went outside to the porch, the neighbor's cat strolled on the porch, meowing for food.

"Hi kitty."

The grey cat purred and rubbed against my leg.

"Are you hungry?" I kneeled down to pet the cat.

"Yes I am," Victor chuckled.

He seemed to have appeared from nowhere, this was becoming a habit of his, always sneaking up on people.

"Hey, where did you come from?"

"I saw you come out. ---So who is your friend?"

"This is the neighbor's cat, he always comes for leftovers."

Victor reached to pet the cat.

The cat snarled at him and ran away.

"I guess he doesn't like me," Victor said.

"I guess not," I chuckled.

"I'm glad you like me," he said.

"How do you know I do? I could be putting up a front and in reality I despise you," I said with a straight face.

He kept quiet for a moment and stared at me. His penetrating gaze melted my heart, "little liar," he smiled.

I grinned.

"Amber, do you have a birthmark?"

"Why do you ask?" Suddenly a sense of terror came over me, I found myself reliving my dream as bits and pieces of it slowly appeared in my mind. Then I remembered everything vividly. It could not be, I said to myself, but his question had just confirmed it.

"Do you?" He insisted.

I walked to the other end of the porch. "No."

"You don't?"

"No," I repeated hiding the truth. I was not going to let him know I did. I needed more time to learn about him, and to find out exactly what he wanted besides me. I closed my eyes and remembered more details of that dark dream. I was in a field, there was a dark creature chasing me. I remembered that my name was of significance to him, but my birthmark was meaningful and crucial to this search, but I hid until the dark creature found me and uncovered his face, it was Victor and that was the first time I saw his face in my dream, beautiful and mysterious. I felt a drawing power, like a magnetic force pulling me toward him as I floated in mid-air and he grabbed me. I let myself go even though I feared him. He held me in his arms as I looked into his eyes and heard my heart slowly fading away until it stopped and I was dead.

I opened my eyes, suddenly, everything was making sense, the name, the birthmark, the reason he wanted us to be close. I was the reason he had come to Virginia; he had come for me or for my soul. I was deep in thought.

"What are you thinking?"

"Uh... nothing."

"Did your mom tell you we are going out tonight?"

"Yes, she did," I gulped thinking that if I was right, this could be my last meal but I could not let him take me yet, I wanted to stay with my mother until the end, then after that it would be ok if I died.

However, I did want to confirm if my dream was true. Has he really come for me? Was my time up? Was he really the angel of death? But I did not ask, because deep inside, the fact that he could be the angel of death did not bug me at all, maybe it would bother someone else, but not me. I was expecting him but just not yet, besides I had feeling for him, deep feelings. I sighed and then curiously asked about his midnight escapades maybe I was not the only soul he was there to collect, "Where do you go at night?"

"What?" He asked confused.

"Where do you go? I've seen you and your family leave almost every night."

"Are you spying on us?" He asked unsmiling.

I turned away from him, "Is just that… I have seen you guys leave and come back home late at night and you don't take your car."

"You shouldn't be spying —you're bound to see something you don't want to."

I gulped, "Like what?"

I turned quickly, when I felt him standing right behind me.

He looked upset, "you'll see one day," the tone of his voice was cold, and his stare was intimidating. He stood close to me in a disheartening way; I could feel his cool breath when he talked.

"You are scaring me," I said and pushed him away.

"Good," he grinned.

I walked away.

He put his hands on my shoulder.

I turned, "Victor, no! ---people are starting to talk. My mom and I just last night had an argument about that."

"I know, she told me, and I talked to her and she is ok with us seeing each other."

"Yeah but just like friends, nothing more."

"That's not what she said when I asked her if I could start dating you."

"You did what?" I felt my jaw dropped. I know my mom, and I do not think she would have agreed, at least not until I was older. "My mom is not ok with us dating, are you kidding me," I said alarmed and thinking back to what she had said earlier.

"Yes, she is---, she said it was ok, as long as I respect you, and I promised her I would."

"I have to go back in," I was incredulous.

"Did I upset you?"

"Well don't lie to me, she said this morning that it was ok to talk to you, she never said anything about us dating."

"I'm not lying, go on ask her."

"Maybe I will." I said in a sharp tone, I stared into his eyes, and he seemed to be telling the truth. He never made an effort to try to stop me from asking my mother. But in reality, I was not going to ask her, I did not have the courage. But if in fact she was ok with me dating Victor, something was wrong; maybe her illness had something to do with her mood swings. Her odd behavior really concerned me. "I'll see you later, Victor." I reached for the doorknob.

He grabbed my arm. "Wait! --have you finished reading your book?"

I turned to face him, "Not yet I just started reading it last night, why?"

"I wrote you a poem on the last page."

I looked at him tenderly and smiled softly, "you did? I didn't know you like to write poems."

"I don't, but you inspired me," he held my hand.

"Victor," I murmured and lower my head.

He leaned closer to rest his forehead against mine, and with his free cold hand slowly caressed my face.

"My precious Amber," he whispered.

I closed my eyes for a few seconds, before that precious moment I was living was snatched away when I heard my mom shout my name from inside the house.

"Amber, where are you?"

I jumped back as if I had been electrocuted and I glanced at the door, "coming mom," I shouted back and returned my eyes to Victor, "I have to go, — see you tonight," I gave him a coyly smile.

"I can't wait," he said and took a couple of steps back. Then gave me, a sweet and heart warning smile.

I stood with the door partially open, "Bye."

"Bye," his eyes sparkled with elation.

I went inside to help my mother. She did not even noticed, that I had been talking with Victor on the porch.

Later in the day, my mother and I went to get her clothes from the cleaners.

My mother found Victor's wallet on the driver side. "Is this Victor's?"

"It must be. I'll give it back to him," I held his wallet in my hands.

We finally got back home after finishing the errands. I still had the wallet in my hands, when my mom was not looking I opened it, and sneakily went through it; I saw his driver's license, a lot cash, and a couple of credit cards. Sticking out behind his driver's license was a folded photograph, I carefully pulled it out to see who it was, and it was a picture of me. I was astounded. It was something I was not expecting to find. I had no idea when he took it.

"What are you doing?" My mom caught me looking through Victor's wallet.

"Nothing, I was making sure it was his," I said uneasy.

"I have to go back; the lady at the cleaners gave me the wrong clothes. Some of these are not mine," My mother carried the plastic covered shirts and pants in her arm. "Why don't you take Victor his wallet?"

"Ok," I headed out the door and then turned to my mom, "do you want me to go with you to the cleaners?"

"No, I'll be right back."

"Ok." I crossed the street. I noticed the cars in the driveway. I reached the door and noticed that the door was ajar, someone must have left it unlocked, I knocked on the door, but no one came, then I slowly pushed the door open. I peeked in, "Hello, Victor," I said softly. I was feeling a little nervous for intruding in someone's house like that, but he did it, why could not I?

I heard voices coming from the back room. It was Victor and someone who sounded like his sister. It sounded like they were disagreeing on something, they were not shouting but their voices were loud enough for me to hear.

I then heard Victor say, "She is too young. I can come back for her when she is older."

I listened closely and walked slowly and cautiously toward the voices.

"Do you want to lose her? --and then what, start to look for her all over again, ---why give her up when you have found her?"

"What if is not her?" He said despondent.
"Do you still have doubt? Emma asked.
"I don't know, ---my heart says she is the one, ---I think she is lying about the birthmark," Victor said distressed.
"Ok then..." She said soothingly. "Victor she is getting close to you, let her fall in love ---if she isn't already."
I had reached the room where they were in. Emma was facing the door and saw me come in.
She pointed toward me and lowered her head.
Victor briskly turned around and saw me.
"Uh... the door was open, ---hmm Victor you forgot your wallet in my mom's car."
Victor looked irritated.
"Here," I said dejectedly and placed the wallet on the table near where I was standing and quickly turned around to leave. I could see in his expression that I was not welcome, maybe I heard too much.
"Amber, wait!" Victor said.
"I'll leave you guys alone," Emma walked out of the room.
"Let's go to the patio," he said.
I sensed his bitterness.
"I can't stay long," I was a little apprehensive.
We walked to the patio in the back.
I was nervous, but I tried to start a conversation to calm him down, "Oh, you have a pool."
"Do you want to go swimming?" The tone of his voice was still cold.
I giggled, "Hell no. Are you crazy? That water is probably freezing," I said feeling uneasy. The thought of him drowning me crossed my mind. I gulped.
He laughed. "Thank you for bringing my wallet back." He was his old self again.
"You're welcome," I said relieved. I guess he was not mad. I must have misread him. He probably was just trying to torment me, knowing that I get scare easy, I thought to myself.
"Did you look inside?"
Shamefaced, I answered quickly, "No."
He chuckled. "Are you ready for tonight?"
"Yes," I paused. "Were you guys talking about me?" I asked

warily.

"No."

I did not believe him. I knew they were talking about me. He did have feelings for me. I grinned.

"You shouldn't have sneaked in like that."

"I called your name, but no one answered."

"Hmm," he gave me a disapproving look.

"Why do you have a picture of me in your wallet? ---when did you take that?" I was dying to know.

"Oh... I thought you said you hadn't look." He raised his left eyebrow.

I bit my lips, "Well I had to look to see who it belonged to."

"Sure," he said implausible.

"Are you mad? Don't be," I eagerly leaned closer to him to steal a wild fast kiss.

"Don't do that," he said and held me back.

"I am sorry, I thought..." My voice cracked, "I guess I was wrong," I ran out of his house ashamed with my heart and ego crushed. I ran to my house, I had just made a fool out of myself, he did not like me the way I thought he did, he was just playing with my feeling. They were not talking about me, I felt so stupid to think that.

I saw Brad walking by.

"Hey Amber, hold on... What's the rush?" Brad stopped me.

"Hey Brad."

"Hey, what are you doing?" He asked.

"Uh ---nothing."

Victor's indifference hurt me in a way no one had hurt me before. I was destroyed and unwanted.

I saw Victor walk out of his house and stand on his driveway. I wanted to get him back for hurting me, show him I didn't care about him either.

"Hey Brad, do you want to come in?" I said trying to act enthusiastic.

"Sure, is your mom home?"

"No," I answered.

Brad smiled.

I let him inside the house and we walked to the living room.

"Where is your mom?"

"She is running an errand."

"So we are alone, ---cool," Brad smiled.

There was a loud banging on the door. "Amber, open up!" Victor shouted angrily from the other side of the door.

I opened the door slightly.

He pushed me aside and barged in. "What is he doing here?" His expression was fierce and terrifying.

"He is my friend and I can have a guest if I want to, ---and why do you care? It's none of your business anyway," I said feisty.

"Where is your mom?" He asked fumingly, his eyes were getting red with anger.

"She is not here," I answered hostile, bothered by his presence.

"Get him out of here now," Victor barked.

Brad walked out of the living room to where we were standing after hearing Victor shouting.

Victor stood rigid. "Get out of here Brad," he raised his voice.

I could see the fury in Victor's eyes.

"Dude chill out, what's wrong with you?" Brad raised his voice.

"Amber, tell him to leave…" Victor stared indignantly at me, he then continued. "Now!" he demanded.

I saw the look on his face, he was mad but I could see that I was hurting him too. Mission accomplished, I thought. "Victor you need to go," I said, I wanted to get back at him some more.

He stared at me in disbelief. He then narrowed his eyes and scoffed, "no. ---I am not leaving until he does."

I stood defiant in front of him.

Victor grabbed my arm, and walked me to the side. "Look at me, get him out before I kill him," he uttered.

I did not want to be the reason why Brad would lose his soul prematurely, so I agreed. "Ok…" I said to Victor. I then turned to Brad, "Brad you have to go, my mom is not here and she is going to kill me if she knows I let a guy in the house when she wasn't home."

Brad scoffed and shook his head, "I see how it is. It is ok that he stays, but I can't? ---you know what just forget it Amber ---I'll see you later," he said chagrined.

"Bye, Brad. I'm sorry."

Brad let himself out and slammed the door.

"Are you happy now?" I screamed at Victor.

"What the hell are you thinking?" Victor reproached me.

"Me? You, you are the one acting weird, ---you want me, and then you don't want me. I don't get you," I yelled confused with my arms up in the air frustrated. "Argh!"

"Amber, it's that…"

I was disillusioned, "just go Victor," I opened the door.

"Are we still on for tonight?"

"Are you serious?" I scoffed, "I don't even know if I want you as my friend anymore."

"Don't say that," he said with a grim twist of the mouth, "lock the door, please."

"Yes… Dad," I said patronizingly and rolled my eyes. I slammed the door behind him and pressed my back against the door. I was demoralized. I wanted him out of my head, out of my heart, but it was so hard, I hated it this feeling, I hated being in love.

I started to pick up downstairs before my mother got back; I had to face her to let her know I was not in the mood of going to dinner. I took the rest of the clothes that my mother had brought from the cleaners to her room.

I then went to my room. The lights in the room were off. I reached for the light switch but it did not work, I clicked it a couple of times.

"Damm it! ---the light bulb burned," I mumbled to myself.

I walked to the nightstand to turn on the lamp.

Brad was lying on my bed and startled me. I jumped, "What the…"

He sprung off the bed, grabbed me by the wrists, and shoved me in the bed.

"What are you doing?" I struggled with him trying to free myself, his husky physique controlling my movements.

"I am doing exactly what you want? He fondled me. "Do you like that, huh?"

The tone of his voice was vulgar and nasty.

"Stop it! Get off me! What's wrong with you?" I squirmed trying to break free from this obnoxious idiot, but he held my wrists tighter and pinned me down to the bed. I could feel his hands under my shirt, the feeling of repulsion was too strong, and I felt my stomach doubled up as he continued to touch me. Then with his free hand, he started to unzip my jeans. I continued to kick my legs. I wanted his filthy hands off me.

"Stop Brad!" I yelled angrily, but I could see in his eyes that he was not going to stop.

He slobbered kisses all over my face. A minute of his torture felt like an eternity in hell.

I shook my head from side to side trying to avoid him kissing my mouth. I was disgusted my stomach twisted for the hundredth time. I was feeling sick.

Brad finally managed to unzip my jeans.

"Victor," I screamed his name, but then Brad shut me up with a nasty kiss.

Tears rolled down the side of my face as he kissed my neck. I closed my eyes, wishing this nightmare would end. I continued to struggle, telling him to stop. I kicked some more trying to free myself from under him. I was not going to go down without a fight, I bit his ear, and it started to bleed.

"Ouch! --you little slut!" Brad covered his bleeding ear. He then raised his other hand in the air ready to slap me.

Suddenly, Victor appeared at the end of the bed, I could barely see him, my eyes were glossy with tears, but there was something strange about him, his eyes were black with a threatening and fearless look. His face looked evil and dangerous.

He picked up Brad like a rag doll and threw him across the room.

Brad's body crashed like a thunder against my bedroom wall. Brad's body lay unconscious on the floor.

I jumped up and zipped my jeans, my hands were shaking. I wiped my mouth with my shirt.

Victor looked at me concerned, "Are you ok? Did he…?"

"No, he didn't," I said with weeping tears.

"Come here," he said and offered me his arms to comfort me.

"Is he ok? --is he dead?"

"Why do you care if he is ok? ---after what he did, he should be dead. Amber he was going to rape you, if I had not heard you."

"You heard me?" With teary eyes, I looked at him incredibly.

His hazel eyes looked normal once more.

"I am glad you are ok, I just wish I had gotten here sooner."

"Thank you... and I'm sorry, ---I should have listened to you," I cried and buried my face against his chest; I could feel his chiseled muscles contouring his upper body.

His cold hand lovingly touched my face.

I stared deeply at him; I wanted to know the truth. "What are you, Victor?"

"You don't want to know..." He paused, "...at least I don't think you are ready yet."

"But I am. I want to know the truth."

I heard a man's voice. "Ahem... may I come in?" He grinned.

"This is Max," Victor said to me.

Max had curly black hair, brown eyes, and the same pale skin as the rest of his family; Max had climbed the trellis outside my window and was squatting on the edge of the window.

They both stared at me, waiting for my response.

"Aren't you going to invite me in?" Max asked me.

"Oh yeah, get in before you fall and kill yourself," I said.

They both laughed.

"What happened? Max asked.

Victor explained to him what just had happened.

Max looked at Brad's motionless body, "Is that him?"

"Yeah, get rid of him," Victor told him.

"Do you want me to really get rid of him?" Max questioned. A malevolent grin appeared on his face.

Victor glanced at me. "It's your call."

My eyes widened in shock, "No, don't kill him."

"Ok, I'll do what you say, but I wish you hadn't say that," he gave me a judgmental look. He then turned to address Max, "just dump him somewhere, let him freeze in the cold, ---he is not going to gain consciousness anytime soon and if he does give him a good scare."

Max went to pick up Brad's motionless body and saw that his ear was bleeding, "oh I see she has been practicing," he grinned and threw him over his shoulder.

"What?"

"Nothing, don't mind him." Victor motioned Max to go.

I sat on the corner of the bed, and watched how easily Max

jumped out the window with Brad's limp body on his back, as if he was a wet noodle.

Victor sat next to me.

I hesitated, "Victor, ---you are not human, are you?"

"No."

I already suspected this, but I still got chills in the back of my neck, "Do they know?"

"Who?"

"Your family?"

He chuckled, "Yes." Then he paused when he saw the fear reflecting in my eyes, "...I don't want you to be afraid of me. You need me and I need you."

"But what are you?"

"I can't tell you, just not yet, I don't think you are ready." He looked away, "let's not talk about it anymore, ok?"

I had so many questions, was he really the dark angel, was Max some sort of his sidekick, but I was afraid to ask him, I wanted him to open up to me, "don't you trust me with your secret?" I put my hand on his shoulder.

"I will tell you, I promise, but only when the time is right," he turned to me and smiled tenderly.

His smile lighted up my soul, it was impossible for me to say no. "Ok." I nodded.

He held my hands and said, "I want to apologize for acting so cold to you earlier. I get excited when you get near me and you sort of caught me by surprise and I didn't want you to see me that way," he explained.

The mystery behind him was driving me crazy. Even though, I wished I knew the truth, I was still afraid of the unknown.

"See you how? Do you mean like a few minutes ago, when you threw Brad across the room?"

"You saw me?" he glanced down ashamed.

"Yes, sort of... your face changed," I looked at him deeply waiting for his reaction.

"And... do I scare you?" he asked grim-faced.

"Yes," I looked away remembering parts of my dream, I couldn't stand it no more and I went ahead and asked, "Are you going to kill me?"

He chuckled, "What? Where did you get that idea?"

I smiled bashfully, "Well ---before I met you I had a…" I stopped immediately when I heard a car pull up in our driveway.

He turned around alerted and walked to the window.

"Is that my mom?"

"I'm afraid so," he peeked through the curtains out the window. "Yes, that's her," he confirmed.

"I am dead meat, if she finds you here," I said in a panicking voice.

"She won't."

I heard the front door open.

"Amber, I'm home," My mom shouted from downstairs.

I stood next to Victor.

I was panicking, "Please don't tell her what happened," I spoke softly.

"Why not? He needs to be punished."

"Shh… she is going to hear you," I watched the door and glanced back at him, "How am I going to explain to her about you and Max, huh?" I ran my fingers through my hair feeling frantic.

"Ok, I won't say anything."

"Thank you…" I smiled, "go, she is coming."

Wait he leaned toward me and gave me a small peck on the corner of my mouth.

"You missed," I grinned.

"No, I meant to do that… I'll kiss you when the time is right."

Even though, I did not know for sure what he was, the thought of him kissing me, made me feel like I was in cloud nine. I could feel my cheeks turning beet red. "But isn't the timing right? ---the hero saves the damsel in distress and he kisses her and they live happily ever after."

"This is not a fairytale, and I'm not your hero, I'm more like your predator."

His words gave me goose bumps.

"I'll see you later," he said with a grave expression on his face.

There was a knock at the door, "Amber, are you in there?"

"Coming mom," I turned back to Victor to hurry him up, but he was already gone.

I opened the door.

"Look what I got you for tonight," My mother showed me a

dress she had bought for me.

The dress was hideous; the only place I could see myself wearing that was to my funeral and that would be because I would not be able to dress myself. "Nice," I grinned politely. I did not want to hurt her feelings.

"You don't like it?"

"Hmm... not really," I giggled.

"Ok, I'll return it tomorrow." She tried the light switch, "what's wrong with your light?"

"I need to change the light bulb."

"Well there are some in the storage cabinet in the laundry room."

"Ok, I'll get it. Did they find your clothes, mom?" I asked, holding the door, hoping my mother did not notice anything else messed in the room.

"Oh yes, that poor lady I gave her an earful." She chuckled. She noticed my messy hair, "I thought you would have taken a shower by now."

"Sorry, I got sidetracked." I hated lying to her, but I had to.

"Ok, well hurry up and start getting ready; they are going to be here in an hour."

"Yes mother," I said playful and blew a kiss at her, "Love you."

She snickered, "Love you too."

Mr. and Mrs. Cromwell picked us up; Victor was waiting inside the smoky gray Range Rover.

My mother and I sat in the back, next to Victor. I was in the middle between my mom and Victor.

My mother is very sociable; with her there, I knew I did not have to do much talking.

We arrived at Chez Vous and waited to be seated.

"You are not talking much," I said to Victor.

He smiled and leaned to whisper in my ear, "I am observing it has been a while."

"Oh."

The hostess took us to our table, which was secluded in a corner of the restaurant. She gave us the menus, and we ordered.

Victor was sitting next to the left of me.

I saw Victor's expression when they brought the plates. It

was priceless.

His steak was rare, the same way his mom and dad had asked for theirs.

I tried not to stare at him, but it was funny seeing him having trouble eating his steak.

He did not even bother to touch the vegetables. He had a look of disgust on his face, as if he was getting sick.

"Don't eat it," I whispered to him.

He put his fork down.

I stopped eating too, so he would not be alone.

"You are not eating, Amber?" My mother noticed.

I smiled, "I am full."

My mother then looked at Victor, "You too Victor?" She asked.

"Yes, I thought I was hungry, but I am not," he replied.

"Kids," my mother said and continued her conversation with Mr. and Mrs. Cromwell.

Victor and I sipped on our drinks. We sat silently listening to the adults' conversation; and occasionally glance at each other while we held hands under the table.

Mr. and Mrs. Cromwell really seemed to like my mom, but then again who would not like her, she was very friendly.

On our way back to the house, Mrs. Cromwell asked my mom permission to take me skiing.

"She doesn't know how to ski." My mother replied.

"Well there are other things to do, ---plus we can give her some lessons," Mrs. Cromwell said.

"Please mom," I begged.

"When is the trip?" My mother asked Mrs. Cromwell.

"Next weekend, after Amber's birthday," Mrs. Cromwell answered.

"We'll all be there. I'll make myself responsible for her," Mr. Cromwell assured my mother.

"Hmm, honey do you really want to go?"

"Yes please," I said eagerly.

"Ok then, is a yes," My mother agreed.

"Thank you, mom," I smiled pleased.

This was the first time she was letting me sleep outside of the house without her.

"We will leave Friday afternoon and come back Sunday evening," Mr. Cromwell added.

"Ok, that sounds good."

We arrived home; they dropped us in front of our house. Victor got out of the car with us.

"Mom, can I stay out for a little bit?" I asked my mother.

"Don't be long." She answered.

Down the street you could see the cars parked outside Chloe's house and the music blasting.

We both looked out that way.

"Are you going to go?" I asked Victor.

"No, not interested. I had a great time tonight... I don't want to ruin it," he stared at me, "By the way you look beautiful, sorry I couldn't tell you sooner. I didn't want to upset your mom."

I grinned bashfully.

"Shy little girl," he smiled softly.

"I am not a little girl," I said offended.

He laughed, "Ok, whatever you say," he continued, "thanks for covering up for me at the restaurant."

"You didn't like the food," I stated.

He made a face of disgust, "Not really."

"Well sometimes that happens to me too, ---thank you for not telling my mom about Brad."

"I want you to promise me, you'll stay away from him."

"I promise, but what if he comes back," the thought of Brad coming back made my skin crawl.

"Don't worry, I'll be watching. Just make sure you lock your bedroom window, ok?"

"But then how would you come in?"

"Just lock it, alright."

"Ok."

Victor softly touched my face with the back of his cold fingers.

I leaned my face toward his touch. His eyes captivated my gaze, I felt warm inside.

He slowly tilted his head down; he brushed soft kisses across my lips; his velvety lips barely touching mine. He did this a few times.

I could not believe he was kissing me, finally, I said to

myself.

"Victor, wait."

"Yes?" He mumbled in between kisses.

I pressed my hand on his chest and held him back, "What happened to that girl, the one you like?" I prayed she was out of the picture.

He pressed his finger against my lips to silent me and smiled. "Shh... she is right here with me," he leaned closer and held my chin up, placing soft gentle kisses all over my lips.

I was dumbfounded. I closed my eyes and drifted away, letting all my feelings flow. I was feeling warm and dreamy; I could feel my heart leaping out from my chest. I was experiencing something I had never felt before. His soft gentle kisses were torturing me, I wanted more than what it felt to me like butterfly kisses.

The porch light turned on.

I stepped back startled by the light. "That's my clue, I have to go in." I chuckled.

My mother opened the door, "Amber, time to come in."

"C'ya," I said to Victor.

Victor continued to stare at me as if he was in a trance. From his expression, I knew he had experienced the same thing I had, a brief moment of pure ecstasy.

I smiled coyly.

"Goodnight Victor," My mother said and pulled me in breaking the spell.

Victor blinked a couple of times, he then looked at my mom, "Goodnight, Mrs. Ross," he returned his eyes back on me, "Goodnight Amber," he had a conquering expression and jubilant smile on his face.

My mom closed the door and leaned her back against it, "take it slow Amber." She looked concerned, "---go to your room."

I gave her a bewildered look, wondering if she had seen Victor and me kissing. I felt guilty, I didn't want to let her down especially now that she was trusting me, but with Victor in the picture and the way I felt about him, it was going to be almost impossible to keep my purity pledge.

"Goodnight, mom," I gave her a goodnight kiss before going to my room.

CHAPTER 5

I woke up startled by the loud beeping sound from the smoke detector. I jumped out of bed, wearing my pink camisole top and heart-print pajama pants. I opened the bedroom door and I sniffed the air. I immediately began to cough when the bitter burn smell hit me jerking my eyes wide open. I called out for my mother and dashed downstairs, the house was permeable with the terrible burned smell. There was a cloud of smoke coming from the kitchen and I went to investigate. The pancakes on the stove were burning. The skillet had caught on fire. The thick smoke in the air irritated my eyes and throat. I coughed a couple of times, before I reached the knob turning off the stove and with lightening fast reflexes I grabbed the skillet and threw it inside the kitchen sink and let the water flow. A big cloud of steam rose, while the lingering smoke brought tears to my eyes.

In the hazy room, I noticed that my mother lay unconscious on the floor.

I kneeled down next to her trying to wake her up, "Mom, mom, are you ok?" I anxiously asked. "Mom, wake up," I shook her.

She was not responding.

I panicked and ran to Victor's house to get help, feeling the cold pavement on my bare feet.

I rang the doorbell and knocked desperately.

Max opened the door, "Amber, what's wrong?"

"I need help, where is Victor?"

"Come in," Max stepped aside.

"No, --come with me," I grabbed Max's hand in desperation and pulled him out of the house, and dragged him to my house for his help without explaining.

Max saw my mother on the floor and ran to help her.

I kneeled beside him and we tried in vain to wake her up.

She did have a pulse and was breathing.

I heard Victor anxiously calling my name.

"We are in the kitchen," Max said.

Then Victor and Mr. Cromwell rushed inside the kitchen, "What happened here?" Victor asked.

"I woke up and the house was full of smoke, when I ran down here I found her unconscious."

"Is she..." Victor started to say.

"No, she is alive," Max said but did not turn to look at Victor.

Then my mother slowly tried to open her eyes, but fainted again.

I held her hand and kissed it, "We need to get her to the hospital," I begged Victor.

Victor sent Max to go get the car. Then Victor scooped my mother up in his arms, carried her outside to the car and rested my mother on the back seat.

I sat next to her while I propped up her head on my lap. I gently rubbed her head, waiting for her to open her eyes and respond to my touch.

Victor and Max took us to the hospital. Once we got to the emergency room, my mother was rushed to a room. I waited impatiently outside the room. I glanced at Victor and Max, who were in a deep conversation a few feet away from me. Mr. Cromwell and his wife arrived shortly after we did and stopped to talk to Victor.

Mrs. Cromwell walked to where I waited desperately and sat next to me. She hugged me in a motherly way, "don't worry she is going to be alright."

I did not even flinched when her cold hand touched my shoulder, "she is not, I know--- she already told me she is going to die," I started to cry.

Mrs. Cromwell rubbed my back trying to soothe the pain I was feeling, "aren't you cold? Where is your jacket?" She looked down at my feet, "--and where in the world are your shoes?" She smiled.

The red lipstick she wore spiced up her smile, making her pale skin look even brighter in the well-lit hospital.

My hands and feet were so cold that they were starting to feel numb, "I forgot to grab them; ---we were in a rush. ---but I'm not that cold." I lied while my whole body shivered.

"Sure you aren't, ---look at you, you are shaking."

Mrs. Cromwell motioned Victor to come, "Victor, why don't you take her home to change?"

"No," I said firmly. "I'm ok."

"Amber, we'll stay here until you come back," Mrs. Cromwell offered.

Victor extended his hand to take me with him.

"No, I need to know that she is ok," I stared in despair at Victor.

Victor gazed at me, his mesmerizing eyes full with compassion, as he understood my fear. He turned his eyes to Mrs. Cromwell and shook his head, "No, Mom."

"But she is cold," Mrs. Cromwell stated.

Victor courteously took his jacket off, and sat next to me. "Here, take my jacket."

Mrs. Cromwell helped me put it on, lifting my hair from my shoulders.

"There you go…" She paused, and touched the back of my shoulder. She continued, "…isn't that much better?"

I turned my head to look at her, "Yes, thank you." I noticed she was grinning and staring at Victor.

"Victor, can you come with me for a second?" Mrs. Cromwell asked him.

Victor looked intrigued; "Sure," Victor followed his mom.

I sat there waiting for the doctor or the nurse to come talk to me, I clutched Victor's jacket trying to warm up my body, but my bare feet were still extremely cold. I curled up my toes trying to make the blood circulate through my feet.

Victor and Mrs. Cromwell were talking secretively. They

would glance at me now and then making it obvious they were taking about me. Mrs. Cromwell had an enthusiastic expression, the same expression she had the first time she met me. I observed Victor while he talked to her; he appeared to be serious and uncertain. He then turned his gaze toward me and stared for a long time in a chastising way as if I had done something wrong.

I was feeling uncomfortable and self-conscious. I looked away, then I saw the doctor and the nurses come out of my mother's room. I rushed to the doctor and stopped him. "Doctor is she going to be ok?"

"Are you her daughter?" The doctor asked.

"Yes."

"She is awake now, she has been asking for you."

"What was wrong, was it the smoke?"

"She did inhale smoke, but that was not the reason she was unconscious. Some of her organs are beginning to fail," the doctor explained and with a sorrowful look on his face he continued, "the cancer has spread to her major organs and she is not reacting to the treatment, there's not much we can do, but she will need to stay a few days until she is stable."

I felt light headed. My knees gave in. I immediately felt Victor's arms around me helping me regain my balance.

Mr. Cromwell also came to help me stay up on my feet. Suddenly, all of them surrounded me. Victor and Mr. Cromwell stood next to me like two strong standing pillars holding the fragile little doll, while Max and Mrs. Cromwell stood close by listening to the doctor.

I continued to talk to the doctor. "Do you know how long she has?" I asked.

"I think your mother is capable of telling you herself."

"Please doctor, ---I know my mom, she won't tell me," I begged.

He sighed giving in, "not long she is going fast, perhaps a few month sweetie."

My eyes welled up with tears. I felt as someone was slowly ripping a part of me.

"I am very sorry," the Doctor tapped me on the shoulder and walked away.

Victor hugged me.

I cried uncontrollably as he pressed me against his firm chest.

"Calm down, you can't go in to see your mom like this, you will upset her more," Victor comforted me.

"Victor, she is going to leave me," I snuggled in his sweet embrace.

I could feel his arms tighter around me.

"She will never leave you; even if she dies she will always be with you, ---in your heart."

Mrs. Cromwell stepped forward taking the place of her husband, she pushed my messy bed hair off my face, "come one, we'll go with you."

I nodded and sniffed.

Mrs. Cromwell handed me a tissue to dry up my tears.

Victor released me from his clasp and I went in to see my mom with him and Mrs. Cromwell on my side.

My mother was laying in the hospital bed resting, with a tube going up her nose for oxygen. The tone of her skin was ashy and pasty. I could not hold back the tears; I rested my head on her chest.

Her hand with the I.V. slowly reached to stroke my head. She softly uttered taking a deep breath, "My sweet little girl."

"Mom, ---don't leave me." I sobbed.

"Honey, don't cry. It has to happen sooner or later; I thought I had prepared you for this."

"I'll never be ready, ---take me with you. I want to die too." I sniffed.

She snickered, "don't say that, you have a beautiful life ahead of you."

"But you won't be in it," I looked at her in despair; my eyes filled with tears, my nose runny from crying.

She stared at me with a slight smile on her face, "look at you, you are mess."

I sniffed, and let a small chuckled out, "so are you," I wiped the tears from my face.

"Savannah, you gave Amber a scare, ---she ran out of the house without her shoes," Mrs. Cromwell told my mother.

"Sweetie, you are going to catch something. What am I going to do with you?" She coughed.

"Mom, it's ok, ---I am ok."

"Are you wearing your PJ's?" My mother chuckled when she

noticed by heart print pajama pants.

I smiled.

"I offered to take her home to change but she is stubborn," Victor commented.

"You are telling me? ---I feel sorry for the guy who marries her," My mother snickered.

A broad smile appeared on Victor's face.

Mrs. Cromwell chuckled.

"Amber, please go home and come back later, and next time with shoes," My mother smiled.

I was happy in a way to see that she still had a sense of humor even if she did not have her color back.

"Go home, it's not like I am going anywhere, besides I would like to talk to Estella in private," My mother requested.

Mrs. Cromwell frowned confused.

"I wish your husband was here too, so I could talk to you both." My mother spoke softly.

"Oh… he is right outside," Mrs. Cromwell informed my mother.

"Do you mind getting him? —I would like to ask you both for a favor."

Mrs. Cromwell agreed and went outside to get him.

My mother asked Victor to take me home and look after me. I argued, pouted and frowned, but I had to go. She mentioned again that she needed to talk to Victor's parents in private. I was curious as to why my mother would need to talk to them. I wondered her motives, but the only thing that came to my mind was the kiss from last night, I figured she was going to tell on us. Victor drove me home, but on our way there, he was unusually quiet; normally he is the one trying to make conversation. He was not being himself.

We walked in my house.

"I'll wait for you down here," he said.

"Ok."

"Can I get my jacket back?"

"Oh sure, thank you so much," I said disconcerted trying to figure what was the rush.

Victor was acting strange. "Let me help you," he offered.

Then I realized that Mrs. Cromwell must have seen my birthmark. That was the reason she had touched my shoulder the way she did. She must have told him about it and that would explain his odd behavior, I thought.

I took the jacket off quickly, "That's ok; I've got it," I covered my shoulders with my hair and handed him his jacket.

Victor sighed and stared deeply into my eyes. His hazel eyes pierced my soul. "Amber, I really need to know if it is you."

"I don't know what you mean." I acted gullible.

"I think you do, ---I don't know how you found out."

Here was my chance to confess about my dream to let him know what I knew, that I have wished so bad to die after learning about my mother's illness that now he had come for me, but I wasn't ready to die yet, not until my mom had passed away first.

He continued, "---I am almost positive that you are the one, but I need to confirm this," he mumbled discretely.

"If I am, what's going to happen to me?" I asked worried.

"That is up to me, so are you?"

I gulped. I did not want to answer him because I was not ready to die yet.

He sighed. "Never mind--- I'll be at home, come and get me when you are done," he left upset.

I got ready as fast as I could. I wanted to get back to my mom. I rushed outside. I saw Victor talking to Chloe. The sight of her repulsed me, even more so by seeing her with him.

I interrupted them.

"Victor, can we go?"

"Of course... see you Chloe."

"Like mother, like daughter," Chloe said condescending.

"Don't talk about my mom." I barked.

She snickered, "It's a free country, and I can say anything I want about you or your mom."

I turned around and pushed her hard on the shoulder, "I told you to shut up!"

She caught herself from falling, "you stupid slut! ---the whole school is talking about you."

I snickered, "I don't care, and if I know better you probably started it."

"Whatever slut!" She sneered.

"Look who's talking at least I haven't dated the entire football team like you have."

Our heated exchange of words escalated, I launched at her; I wanted to rip those golden locks from her head, but Victor grabbed me by the waist, my arms swinging I wanted to claw her eyes out.

"Amber let's go, leave her she is not worth it."

"Let's go leave her," she said mimicking Victor. "Your loss Victor, you're pathetic," she said wrathfully.

Victor ignored her and opened the car door, "Amber, please get in the car."

We drove away leaving Chloe standing there peeved.

But she was not the only one, I was still breathing heavily, I was burning inside with fury. I tried to cool down before talking to Victor, then I turned to him, "Victor, don't believe what they are saying about me. Last night was my first kiss; ---I have never been with a boy," I confessed humbly. "My mom... she has never let me date, growing up I couldn't even go to sleepover parties with my friends..."

He interrupted, "I know Amber... I know."

But he did not look at me, he seemed a little upset and his silence worried me, I was afraid what he thought of me. I remembered his butterfly kisses. His silence gave me the chance time to fantasize about that kiss. I got lost in my own little world, images of him and me, popped in and out of my head, for a brief moment I forgot the tragic nightmare I was living with my mom being in the hospital.

When we arrived at the hospital's parking lot, it was back to reality for me.

He stopped the car.

"Victor," I said.

"Yeah?" He answered a little bit dry.

"Do you think my mom can get better?"

"I don't know, I just hope she does... at least to enjoy you a little longer."

"I do too, maybe the doctor is wrong," I lowered my head.

He lifted my chin up.

I gazed at him, his captivating hazel eyes holding my attention, "did you like kissing me last night?"

He snickered, "Yes, very much," he glanced down shamefully, "---although I wanted more," he confessed.

"So did I," I rested my head on the headrest of the leather seat of his car, "are you going to kiss me again?" I grinned.

"Of course."

I turned to him, and he smiled.

"When?"

"How about now?" He grinned and leaned closer. His face a few inches away from mine, he stared at my mouth, "just a little peck, —ok?"

"Ok," I uttered. I closed my eyes and slightly parted my lips and waited for his kiss.

He gently brushed his lips against mine.

"Victor," his name escaped from my lips.

He mumbled, "hmm?"

"Let me kiss you instead," I suggested.

He snickered, "you don't like how I kiss?" He asked surprised.

"No, I didn't say that, ---it's that they are very light and soft, they feel like a butterfly flapping its wings on my lips," I said disappointed. I wanted him to kiss me with passion, —I wanted some tongue action.

He laughed, "and that's all you are going to get, until I know for sure."

"Oh," I shifted my gaze and looked out the car window, "we better go then." No matter how bad I desired to kiss him, I couldn't let him know that his suspicions about me were correct, —I was the one he was looking for. But I figured if he had his secret, I could have mine too, —it was only fair.

"I thought so," he said crushed.

I was anxious to see my mother and got out of the car first and I heard him mumble.

"Little liar."

"What did you call me?" I waited for him by the frontend of the car.

"You heard me," he replied and grinned. Then he took my hand and we walked to the hospital and did not let my hand go until we stood in front of the white door to my mother's room.

She was awake and smiled when she saw us, there was something strange, she did not looked worried or in pain, "Victor, you just missed your parents, they just left. They want you to go home immediately."

"They do?" He asked intrigued.

"Yes," my mother answered.

"Amber?" He looked concerned.

"I'll be ok; don't forget I am with my mom."

Victor looked as confused as I was, "call me if you need anything."

I nodded and smiled.

"Mrs. Ross, I hope you get to feeling better."

"Thanks for all your help Victor, you are a sweetheart, ---I have never met a young man like you."

"It is always my pleasure, Mrs. Ross," he grinned, "see you later Amber."

I waved bye to him, and pouted. I wished I could have given him a kiss instead.

That was one of his many good qualities, he was always concerned and protective of me, it did not matter if I upset him, how bad I treated him or how mad I made him, he was always there for me. I think my mom saw his protective side, and she liked that. I could see she was fond of him, and she approved of his presence around me. I grinned with elation, I felt like I had won the lottery.

I spent the rest of the day with my mother at the hospital. As if the off-white walls, white tiled floors and the hospital smell were not depressing enough, I had to watch over her when she sleep not knowing if that was going to be the last breath she would take.

My mother woke up and begged me to leave, but I refused.

Later, I went to the waiting area, bought some chips and a soft drink from the vending machine and then came back to the room.

"Sweetie, is that all you are going to eat?"

"I'll get a sandwich later from the cafeteria, don't worry about me... do you want anything?"

"Yes, I want to get out of here," she smiled.

She still did not look too good, but she was smiling which was a good thing.

I wanted to stay the night with her. I nagged, pleaded and begged some more, until she gave in and I stayed there the night watching over her.

A nurse came in, in the morning to check on my mom. I got up to wash my face and rinse my mouth; I got out of the bathroom and was surprised to see Victor walking in. He had showed up at the hospital with a floral arrangement and a white teddy bear with balloons.

"Hi," I smiled.

"Hey, you are not going to school today?"

"Nah… I am going to stay here," I smiled again, "I see you have your hands full, put them on that table, I know she will love them ---thank you!"

"Only one is for her… this one is yours," he handed me the teddy bear with the balloons. "Happy Birthday!" He grinned.

My eyes widened, "Oh my God, it's my birthday I forgot," I giggled.

"Well, I didn't," he gave me a small peck on the cheek.

"Thank you, it's so cuddly," I hugged the fluffy teddy bear.

He smiled, "You are getting more… my mom and my sister each one have something for you… plus I still have a little surprise."

I smiled pleased. "Really? What is it?" I asked curiously.

"If I tell you it won't be a surprise, would it?"

"Amber," My mother said softly.

"Good morning mom, did we wake you up?"

"No. What a pretty bear," she commented.

"Victor brought you flowers, look," I showed her.

"Thank you Victor, they are gorgeous."

The smell and colors of the flowers liven up the dull room.

"Happy Birthday, baby girl."

"Mom, you remembered," I started to cry.

"Oh boy! ---there you go again, stop crying, ---you are going to run out of tears," she teased me. She then continued to say tenderly, "How do you think I was going to forget this special day?"

Victor chuckled, "maybe is because she did."

"No one asked you," I said grouchy.

He laughed.

My mother chuckled, "you forgot?"

"Yeah," I admitted feeling embarrassed.

"Victor, can I ask for another favor."

"Yes, ma'am."

"Can you take Amber to school?"

"Sure."

"Mom, I don't want to go. ---Please don't make me go,

please," I pleaded.

I remembered what Chloe said and the rumors that she said were circulating about me.

My mother hesitated but she let me skip school just because it was my birthday, "but tomorrow you are going, no matter if I am still here in the hospital."

"Sure."

Victor skipped school too and stayed there with us.

Later Mrs. Cromwell and Emma showed up at the hospital with a box from the town Bakery and two gift bags. Mrs. Cromwell and Emma wished me happy birthday. Emma lifted the lid of the box, and exposed a birthday cake with my name inscribed on it and beautifully decorated with pink frosting and white roses.

"Thank you so much," I said and then looked at Victor, who was staring at me and smiling pleased.

"Since we cannot light a candle in here, just close your eyes and make a wish, ok?" Emma said cheerfully.

I closed my eyes, and wished that my mother would get well and could live forever. Then I sat down on the edge of the hospital bed and opened the gifts they brought me. Emma gave me a beautiful blue cashmere sweater and a gift card to a trendy store at the mall. Mrs. Cromwell gave me a bottle of an expensive perfume and a makeup kit.

I was so into the presents that I had not noticed that Victor had sneaked out of the room, "Where is Victor?"

"He'll be right back," Emma grinned.

Victor then walked in with a gift bag, "happy birthday, again."

"Is this the surprise?" I asked with excitement.

"Yes," he answered.

I grinned from ear to ear, and excitedly tore through the pink and yellow gift tissue, and reached inside the bag. I pulled out a music box that was made of a deep green malachite stone with gold artistic inlaid designs adorning the box. It looked like something that belonged in a museum, "wow!" I was speechless.

"Open it," he said enthusiastic.

I did just that, inside it had green velvety lining, and two compartments with gold plated lids.

"Open that compartment," Victor pointed at it.

I carefully lifted the lid, hidden in the compartment was a gold chain necklace with a heart shaped diamond encrusted locket.

"This is beautiful, Victor. It must have cost you a fortune," I pulled it out and admired it.

"No, it's something I have been waiting a long time to give to you," he whispered in my ear.

I gazed at him, and got lost in his eyes.

My mom cleared her throat, "let me see Amber?"

I turned around to show her.

"Victor you have outdone yourself. Wow!" My mother handed me the locket and chain, "What are you waiting for? ---put it on."

"Let me help you," Victor offered and fastened the clasp. "All you need now is a picture of a loved one to put inside, perhaps one of your mom," he suggested and smiled.

"Yes," I grinned at the idea. "I have to find one mom."

"Make sure is a good one," she smiled, "I also have a gift for you, but it's at home," My mother said.

"It's alright mom, you can give it to me later there is plenty of time."

"Don't you want to know what it is?"

"Sure."

She then told me what it was, my birthday could not have gotten any better; waiting for me at home was an eBook reader from her.

I celebrated my birthday in the hospital. It was unusual but Victor and his family made it fun for my mom and me. The cake was delicious; too bad that Victor and his family did not like sweets.

That evening my mother sent me home.

Emma offered to stay with me, but I told her that I would be ok, as long as I had Victor across the street to protect me.

CHAPTER 6

In the morning, Victor took me to school. On our way in, we saw Brad talking to some other kids. He had his arm on a sling and a neck brace, it look like he had been in a car wreck.

The sight of him made my skin crawl.

Victor noticed my reaction, and stared at Brad in a hostile way, "Don't worry he is not going to bother you."

Brad looked intimidated and quickly walked away.

"Did you do that?" I whispered to Victor.

He grinned, "I wish I could have done what I really want to do."

The rest of the school day was a nightmare, although I did not have problems with Brad, I punched a kid in the hallway and was escorted by a teacher to the principal's office after I got into an altercation with two girls in the girls' bathroom. I took a seat in the principal's office, and then the principal walked in.

"Miss Ross, you know what the consequences are for getting in a fight, right?"

"Not really, Sir."

"I am going to have to suspend you for two days."

"But Sir, they started it."

"That's not what I have been told; you shoved one of the girls against a stall and punch the other one in the nose."

"But they started," I repeated.

"How?"

"They were calling me names."

"Well that's not an excuse; name calling does not justify your actions, Miss Ross. You seem like a good girl, and from the lack of information in your folder, you must have never been in trouble, in here or any other school. There must be something that's making you act up this way, ---are you having problems at home?" He asked concerned.

"No, sir."

"Well, I have to call your mother so she can come and pick you up."

"She can't sir, she is in the hospital. I'll walk home."

"I thought you said you weren't having problems at home?" He peeked above his reading glasses and stared at me.

"I am not," I said with a straight face.

The principal would not let me go home alone before it was time; he asked that I wait until the last bell. I sat in silence as I heard my punishment. He was lenient to me, or so he said, but he could have just let me go with a warning, I thought. Instead, the principal suspended me for one day because I had a clean record. He handed me a suspension slip for my mom to sign. I folded the piece of paper and shoved it in my backpack. After his lecture on how I should behave more like a lady, he told me to wait outside his office until the last bell rang and I could go home. I took a seat just outside his office; I sat there with misty eyes. I was upset, and humiliated. I wanted to cry.

When the bell finally rang, I picked up my backpack from the floor, and I pushed my way out of the school. I just wanted to run home. I busted open the exit door, the glare of the sun hit my eyes, I turned my head and I saw Victor by his car waiting for me. He was the reason why everyone was talking bad about me. I turned around, went back inside and exited out of the side door. I walked home taking a different route so that Victor would not find me. When I got home, I quickly made myself, a peanut butter and jelly sandwich and headed to the hospital before Victor would come on knocking at the front door.

I made it to the hospital, the elevator door opened and I stepped out on the third floor, where my mom's room was.

Victor saw me and quickly walked toward me, "Where have you been, I've been looking all over for you?"

"I am here now; I am going to see my mom," I said indifferently.

"Who gave you a ride?"

"No one." I said with a tone of annoyance.

"How did you get here then?"

"Haven't you ever heard of the bus?"

"What's wrong, why are you acting this way?" He asked concerned.

"Nothing, I am tired. I want to see my mom," I said dull and continued walking.

Victor followed me to my mother's room.

I promptly stopped and faced him, "I want to be alone Victor."

"Why?" He seemed hurt.

"Please leave."

He was puzzled, but he complied with my request.

I did not tell my mother I had been suspended, how could I, she had already enough to worry about.

The doctor came in and told us that my mother could be heading home as early as tomorrow. That was the best news I had heard all day. I asked my mom if I could spend the night there, and she let me, as long as I went to school in the morning. And I agreed.

After a while of changing the channels on the TV looking for something interesting to watch, I dozed off. I woke up by my mother's voice. I heard my mother talking. I opened my eyes and saw her hanging up the phone.

"Who were you talking to?" I sat up straight on the chair, and stretched out my back.

"Victor, --he was wondering if you were here, I told him you were going to spend the night, but for him to pick you up in the morning to go to school."

"Mom, why did you do that? I don't want to go with him," I said anguished.

"I needed to make sure you had a ride to school. I certainly can't take you," she paused looking at my anguished expression. "Since when you don't like riding with him, did you guys have an argument, did he tried to have his way with you?"

"No mom!" I scoffed, "Never mind." I crossed my arms in front of me and leaned back. I wished I could confide in her, but I could not.

She dimmed the lights, and lay back in bed.

I kept thinking about Victor. I closed my eyes, and tried to fall asleep, but could not. I tossed and turned fluffing the pillow, but that chair was not a comfortable place to sleep in.

The next morning, I opened my eyes and looked at my watch. It was around six thirty, I looked at my mom and she was still sleeping, I wanted to give her a kiss before I left, but I was going to wake her up, so I sneaked out of my the room, and carefully closed the door. I headed downstairs to the lobby, then I saw Victor walking in to the hospital; I hid in the ladies' room, once I thought he was gone, I opened the door slightly and peeked out. I did not see him, he must have gone upstairs, I thought. I scurried out of the hospital and walked to the nearby fast food place, where I bought some breakfast. I waited there, slowly drinking my orange juice, until it was safe for me to go home.

I had timed it perfectly; I figured that by now Victor would be at the school looking for me. I grinned deviously. I took the transit bus and went home; the closest stop was about four blocks away. I had reached my destination; I finally got down to our block, I could see my house, and obviously, I could see Victor's huge mansion up ahead. There were no cars parked in the driveway.

I thought great! I felt relieved. I was safe, but then the sound of screeching tires coming to a halt startled me; I turned around briskly.

Victor pulled next to me, and got out of the car yelling at me, "What are you doing? Your mom thinks you are in school."

I did not answer and crossed the street to my house, ignoring him.

He got back in his car and pulled in our driveway.

I ran past him and up the couple of steps to the porch to open the front door.

"Amber, talk to me. What's going on?"

I fidgeted with the keys, "Victor, leave me alone."

"Tell me why? Did I do something wrong?"

"You need to stop coming around," I managed to open the door. I went in.

I did not think that people talking about me would affect me so much, but it has. I was crushed I thought that I would be able to ignore all the gossip, but it was hard. I guess I did not have as much of a thick skin as I thought.

Victor held the door and kept me from closing it. He forced his way in and closed the door behind.

"It is best if I don't see you anymore," I said anguished. My heart was breaking, but I needed to be strong if I wanted to end this now before it got more serious and my mom would hear about it, and then she would be the one ordering me to end my friendship with Victor.

"Why?" He asked wretchedly.

I could see that my words had tormented him. I was wordless. I felt an excruciating pain deep inside my chest. I closed my eyes. I was hopelessly in love with him, but I felt like I had to give him up.

"Why are you skipping school?"

"I am not, I was suspended."

"Why? What did you do?"

"I got in a fight with a couple of girls in the bathroom."

"What?" He laughed, "is that why you are upset? ---have you told your mom?"

"It's not funny, and no she doesn't know, ---I don't want to upset her. Those girls were calling me names; I was defending myself."

"Amber, they are just jealous."

"Oh yeah… how about the boy in the hallway that offered me money, if I went with him to the boys' locker room, huh? Was he jealous too?" Tears slowly started to roll down my face.

"Who is he? Tell me, I'll show him not to mess with you again."

"Who cares? ---if it's not him, it's going to be some other kid propositioning me or making crude and offensive comments to me."

"Is that why you are avoiding me?"

"Yes." I raised my voice.

"So just because of that, you don't want to see me anymore." He looked incredulous. "I thought you care for me more than that," he said crushed.

I lowered my head feeling ashamed, "I am sorry, but I'm the one that has to continue to go to that school for two more year, not you, ---beside you don't get the bad rap, you're the stud and I'm the slut," I said anguished.

"Don't say that, you know you are not, and you know I don't think that about you. Amber, I am sorry I have brought you so many problems," he said regretfully.

"You are sorry we met?"

"No, I will never be sorry about that, you?"

"No." I answered.

He smiled, "So are you going to hide here all day until you can go back to the hospital?"

I chuckled, "Yes."

"I don't think it's a good idea, your mom is being discharged this morning, —my parents are bringing her home. What are you going to tell her, when she sees you here?"

"It's this morning? I knew she was getting released but I thought it would be later this afternoon."

"Why don't you come with me, we can spend the day together," he suggested.

"No… no that's not a good idea, we can get in more trouble."

"I'll promise to keep my hands to myself."

I giggled, "It's ok, I'll just hide in my closet until its time, she won't know I'm there, ---unless you tell her."

"I won't, if you promise not to break up with me," he looked at me with those piercing hazel eyes.

"Victor, ---I can't promise that."

I could see I was hurting him.

"I won't let you," he quickly glanced outside, "I should go --- they should be pulling up any moment now," he rushed out the door and sped away in his car.

I ran upstairs to my room and closed the door.

I then heard the front door open, my mother was laughing, her voice sounded healthy and cheerful. I then heard Mr. and Mrs. Cromwell leave. I could hear my mom walking around, there were footsteps near my door, I tip toed to the closet and stayed in there. I finished reading the Romeo and Juliet book; the story really touched me even though I already knew it, I was in tears. I guessed that is what happens when you are in love; everything around you seems so romantic. I turned to the last page and finally read the poem Victor wrote called 'Eternal Love'. In a way, it reminded me of us. The poem was about two misunderstood lonely souls, one searched for the other until they finally met, all they wanted was to love and be loved, but were not able to come together and be happy until they reached the afterlife, where they were reunited finding eternal love.

The hours went by slow. I was so bored; I leaned against the wall and took a nap. I woke up when I heard the doorbell. I looked at the time and it was time for me to be getting home from school. I heard Victor's voice coming from downstairs talking to my mother. I threw my backpack out of the window and proceeded to climb down the trellis, I then jumped once I have gotten close enough to the ground. I picked up my backpack and walked out of the side of the house without being noticed.

My mother and Victor were talking by the front door.

"There she is," My mother pointed at me when she saw me.

"Hi mom," I greeted her with a big smile and I ran to her to give her a hug.

"What took you so long, why didn't you come home with Victor?"

"Yeah, I would like to know that too," he said with irony.

My eyes narrowed into a hostile slits when his eyes met my iced cold glare.

He grinned.

"I didn't see you, and the school bus was loading, so I rode the bus home instead."

He shook his head, and coughed up the word liar.

I proceeded to go inside.

"I'm going to tell on you," Victor whispered to me when I passed by him.

I glanced at him and stuck my tongue out.

He snickered, "I was telling your mom, she is looking better, she got her color back," Victor commented.

"Yes she does," I hugged her. "I'm glad you are back at home."

"So am I. --I can't stand the hospital," My mother said, and then she continued, "Amber, Victor was telling me that Emma is going shopping for the ski trip, and wants to take you. I am going to give you some money so you can get a few things that you need."

"But mom, no... I don't want to go anymore."

Victor raised his eyebrows, "Why?"

My two reasons for not wanting to go were standing before me. I was worried about leaving my mother alone and the less time I spend with Victor it was better, it would make it easier for me to push him away and detach him from my heart.

"I just don't."

"Sweetie, if you don't want to go because of me... don't worry I'll be fine, I feel great. I haven't felt like this in a while, --- plus I want you to have fun, I want to see a smile on this sour looking face," she lifted the corners of my lips with her index fingers to make me smile.

"So you are still coming, right?" Victor asked me.

"Yes she is. Tell Emma she will go shopping with her," My mother answered his question.

"Great!" Victor said, "Amber can I talk to you for a second?"

"Go!" My mom pushed me toward him. "I'll be upstairs." She left us both standing there.

I watched her go upstairs, and I turned to Victor, who was staring at me with a concerned look.

"I really want you to come, put this rumor nonsense aside, please," he begged.

"It's not that easy Victor, ---its better we end this now before we get more involved don't you think?"

Victor tensed up when he heard me said that, he then said very firmly, "no, —not now, —not ever," he rolled his eyes and huffed, "I'll tell Emma to come pick you up." He opened the door and left.

I leaned against the door. I had a feeling of defeat; I feared my heart was not going to let me win this war.

"Amber what's wrong?" My mother had come back downstairs.

"Mom, why are you doing this?"

"Amber, they have been very nice to us, Mr. and Mrs. Cromwell are very fond of you. I have even asked them that when I die if they would like to be your legal guardian until you are eighteen of course."

"You did what? Are you crazy? What... why are you talking

about dying," I raised my voice slightly. My stomach turned hearing her say the word dying.

"Amber, you need to face it. I don't want you to end up in foster care, so if I can find you a good family now that can take care of you, ---I will," She said determined. She continued, "I don't want to see you grow up like me waiting in an orphanage to be adopted."

"Why can't I live alone?"

"You know the school and the neighbors will report you and Social Services will come for you and place you somewhere, where you don't want to be, ---at least with them you have a family, they have money and can take good care of you, and you will still have Victor to protect you."

I was furious at my mom. I clenched my jaw, I was so livid, I had trouble articulating, I took a deep breath to cool down, but it seemed impossible. "You said you talked to them, what did they say?"

"They agreed. They really like you."

My mom has done some strange things in the past, but this one really took the prize. "I'll be in my room," I said frustrated.

"Aren't you going to eat before you go with Emma?"

"No thanks, just call me when she gets here."

Thanks to my mom I had lost my appetite, my stomach felt sour, I wanted to throw up. I dropped my backpack on the floor and slumped into my bed, hoping to get some relief from my burning stomach. I stared at the ceiling, and started to think, trying to see the bright side of this murky mess. Maybe this would be for the best. I would be sort of like Victor's little sister, which would be a good way to stop the feelings I was having for him. It would sure put a stop to all the rumors.

I huffed. I was still mad at my mother. She should have taken into considerations my feelings for Victor. She knew I had more than a crush for him, but she had her crazy reasons for doing this to me. I liked The Cromwells, but they were still strangers to me. The thought of her passing me along like a piece of furniture, made my blood boil, but at the same time was breaking my heart. How could she? I said to myself.

"Amber," my mother knocked and opened the bedroom door, "Emma is here."

"Whoop de do," I mumbled, feeling extremely mad at my mother.

"Amber, I want you to be nice,"

"Yeah I forgot she is going to be my new sister, isn't she mom?" I said curtly.

"Amber, I am doing this for your benefit, it's only until you are eighteen, after that you can do anything you want."

"Sure mom," I rolled my eyes.

"Here is the money, have fun shopping," she handed me the money.

I twisted my mouth in a censured non-responsive way. I unwillingly went shopping with Emma. I saw of couple of things I needed and some I really liked. Emma made me try many outfits, coats, boots and hats; it was like being in a fashion show. Almost every outfit I tried she insisted that I would get it and she paid for the whole thing. I have to admit I did have fun with her too. Emma had a very charismatic and cheerful personality; she made it easy for me to forget my mother's backstabbing.

At the end of our shopping spree, she dropped me by the front door, my hands full with packages; my mother opened the door when she heard the car.

"Goodness, this is a hundred dollars?" She said eyes wide-opened surprised looking at the four bags I was carrying.

"No, more like three hundred, —oh! Here is your money, Emma insisted on paying."

"Huh... I guess you had fun shopping then?"

"Yes I did," I admitted.

She smiled gladly, "well your dinner is on the stove if you are hungry."

"I am not, we ate at the mall."

"Ok."

Then I noticed she was all dressed up in a nice dark blue dress, she had curled her hair, her make-up was a little heavy, but it looked good.

"Where are you going?" I asked.

"Oh, Estella and Aubrey are going to see a play at the Valley Theater and they invited me to go with them," her eyes shined with excitement. "Do I look good?" She twirled for me showing off her dress.

"You sure do, mom," I smiled with joy seeing her happy.

Then the doorbell rang.

My mother excitedly opened the door.

It was Mr. Cromwell, "Ready?" He asked her.

"Yes," she then looked at me, "sweetie don't wait up, remember tomorrow is a school day."

I nodded and smiled, "have fun."

Mr. Cromwell glanced at me, "Goodnight Amber."

"Goodnight."

I locked the door behind them.

CHAPTER 7

I stood in front of the mirror drying my hair, trying to decide if I should go to school or not. I sure did not feel like putting up with more insults, but if I did not go, I know I would get in more trouble than I was already in.

I grabbed a pen from my backpack and forged my mom's signature to the paper the principal had given me for her to sign and hid it between my books.

After breakfast, my mom dropped me at school on her way to work. Miraculously, she seemed to be her old self again.

Victor walked behind me when I was putting my books in the locker.

"Hey," he smiled, "do you need a ride this afternoon?"

"No my mom is picking me up," I shut the locker door and walked away leaving him standing by the locker.

"Amber, wait!" He rushed passed a few kids to catch up.

"What's wrong?" He asked confused.

I pulled him to the side. "Don't talk to me here in school," I whispered.

The bell rang at that moment.

"But why?" He asked.

"You know why. See you later, Victor," I said anguished and rushed to class.

I tried not to go to my locker, just like the first day. I was again avoiding Victor.

On my last class, I eagerly waited for the last bell to ring. I kept watching the clock on the wall as the minutes slowly dragged by. I pretended to work on my assignment when my mind was really miles away; and finally the bell rang setting us free.

I gathered my books and rushed out of class with the rest of the kids —ready to start the weekend. Although I did not have any confrontations today, I was so glad it was over; my only problem now was facing my mom and Victor to let them know I was not going on the trip.

I smiled, when I saw my mom's car waiting for me outside.

My mom honked the horn, and pulled to the curb to pick me up.

I got a glimpse of Victor standing by his car. The same way he did every day when he waited for me to take me home.

"I see Victor is still here," she noticed.

"Yes I saw him." I bent down and pretended to be looking for something in my backpack that I had on the floor between my legs, "How was your day Mom?"

"Good. I went to see an attorney."

"For what?" I sat up straight when she drove away from the parking lot.

"You know, I want to leave everything legal, make sure you have all the documents you need when I die."

"Mom, please stop talking about that," I complained.

"Ok, well how was your day honey?" She said changing the subject.

"Good," I said blandly.

"Wow, what enthusiasm," she said with sarcasm.

My mom pulled up in our driveway and parked the car.

As we walked to the front door, I heard the sound of tires screeching coming to a halt, I turned around and saw Victor exiting his car, which he had parked right behind ours.

"Hello Mrs. Ross."

My mom had her keys in her hand unlocking the door and she glanced at him. "Hello Victor."

He stood by the porch steps, "Amber can I talk to you for a minute?"

"Sweetie don't be long, you still need to pack," My mother said to me.

I exhaled deeply, I still had not told my mom, I was not going, "What is it Victor?"

"Why did you avoid me all day? You didn't go to your locker I waited at the end of every period for you." He seemed puzzled.

"Victor things have changed even more, I ---I really don't think is wise that you continue whatever game you are playing with me."

"I'm not playing any games," he said distressed.

I looked across the street to his house and saw Max and Emma loading their car.

"They are getting ready to go."

He turned and looked at them, "I guess I'll let you go so you can get ready too."

I hesitated, "Uhm Victor, ---I'm not going."

"Why? Your mom wants you to go," he desperately ran his fingers through his hair, "I thought we were done with this conversation," he had an exasperated look on his face.

"I'm sorry. I just don't feel like going."

"Is it because of me or did someone say something to you again?"

Before I could respond, my mother opened the door and stuck her head out, "Amber, come on ---you need to pack."

Victor grinned, "I guess you are going after all," he mumbled.

I rolled my eyes and huffed.

He checked the time on his watch, "We leave in forty minutes, be ready," he said and left.

I then followed my mother back upstairs.

"Honey you need to change. I already started packing for you," she said when we reached the room.

I sat on my bed next to the duffel bag she had been packing, "Mom, I don't want to go."

"Oh no, you are going. I want you to spend some time with them to see how you guys get along." She said in a peeved tone.

"Why mom? They are nice yes, but ---why do you want me to live with them?"

"Do you want to be bounced from home to home without

being able to make any friends, is that what you want or end up in an orphanage until you are 18 and they kick you out?" She folded another sweater and stuffed it in the duffle bag with force. "This is the last time we talk about this. Now go change your clothes, you have fifteen minutes to get ready." Her nostrils flared.

"Argh!!" I exclaimed feeling flustered.

"Honey, just see it like a mini-vacation and have fun."

Nothing that I could say was going to change her mind, I had to go and be miserable the whole weekend, just to please her.

I snatched the beige turtleneck sweater from the bag, "Can I have some privacy, please?"

She turned around.

I finished changing clothes and put on the boots that Emma and I had bought the day before. "Is this better? Are you happy now?"

She turned around to look at me, "Yeah, that's much better… but let your hair loose, don't put it in a pony tail," she undid my ponytail.

"But mom!" I complained. "They won't care how I wear my hair."

"But see how pretty you look with it down, you look more sophisticated."

I sighed angrily and rolled my eyes.

"Come on —I think is time." My mom headed downstairs.

As I walked down the stairs like a lost soul, the doorbell rang. I stopped in the middle of the stairway and rested the duffle bag down on the step.

My mother opened the door and let Mr. Cromwell in.

"Amber, do you need help with that?" He stared at the bag next to my feet.

"No thank you, I can manage," I continued going the flight of stairs, and grabbed my parka from the coat tree by the door.

"Goodbye mom." I said despondent.

"Goodbye sweetie. Have a good time,"

"Don't worry Savannah, she is in good hands," he handed my mother a list of all the cell phones and ways to get in touch with me if she needed.

"Thanks, but who says I'm worried?" She laughed nervously.

He chuckled, "I understand ---first weekend away from you?"

"Yes, you know how it is." She giggled.

"Like I said she is in good hands… we'll take care of her, like she is one of our own."

I listened to them talk about me as if I was invisible. "Bye mom," I repeated.

"Call me when you get there, ok?"

"Sure," I pouted.

"I'll make sure she does," Mr. Cromwell said.

I carried my bag across the street to Mr. Cromwell's car.

Emma and Max were waiting inside Max's car.

I sat behind Mr. Cromwell who was driving. Then Victor came out of the house and threw his jacket in the back of the car. He sat next to me on the other side.

On the drive to the cabin, I refused to talk. I just looked out the window staring at the panoramic view. Mrs. Cromwell asked me a few questions trying to start a conversation, but I only gave her short and polite answers. I caught Victor's reflection on the window as he stared at me. I turned to look at him, but he immediately shifted his eyes away from me. We finally arrived at the cabin about an hour later.

It was a secluded lodge, near the river, with a big porch all around it. Pine trees and snow surrounded it just like a holiday post card.

Emma and Max got out of their car.

"Hey guys, help me take the luggage in," Mr. Cromwell said to Max and Victor; and they went to help.

"Babe, be careful with mine," Emma shouted to Max.

"I don't have it, Victor does," Max answered Emma.

"You mean this one, oops!" Victor acted as if he was dropping it.

"Victor!" Emma shouted and playfully ran after him.

I stood next to the car with my coat on, the crispy icy air blew on my face, as I turned around to look at the snow-capped mountains in the background, the fresh snow made the landscape spectacular but not even the marvel of nature was going to cheer me up.

"Amber, let's go in and set you up, that way you can call your mom." Mrs. Cromwell smiled and hugged me, "You seemed worried on the drive here," Mrs. Cromwell commented as we walked on the white carpet of fresh snow.

"Yes I guess I'm worried about her, sorry." I said over the sound of the ice crunching beneath our steps.

"You don't need to apologize… come on I'll show you were the phone is."

I smiled.

The lodge was furnished with elegant trendy rustic wood furniture. There was a huge stone fireplace in the middle of the room, which had not been lit yet. The loft upstairs overlooked the living room.

Mrs. Cromwell showed me around the place.

There was a pool table upstairs in the game room, and a pinball machine. All the rooms were downstairs except for one at the opposite end of the game room.

I saw Victor walking out of there.

I tried not to stare at him too much but my eyes kept betraying me.

"Did you set her up?" Mrs. Cromwell asked Victor.

"Yes her bag is in there, extra blankets and towels, everything she needs," Victor answered in a dry tone, and gave me a tormented look as he walked passed me.

"That is your room; it has its own bathroom and a phone… that way you can call your mother at anytime in case you are having problems with the cell phone signal."

"Thank you."

She left me alone and I called my mom, but I had nothing to worry, she was ok and happy that we had made it safe. I told her how beautiful the place was, and we had a short talk, then she hanged up. I wished I could have kept her on the phone longer so that I did not need to face Victor and his parents.

Mrs. Cromwell called me to meet her downstairs. She wanted Victor to show me the surrounding near the cabin.

Victor stood by the door, "Come, let me show the river," Victor faked a smile and walked outside.

I followed him only because Mrs. Cromwell was watching me.

"Come it's over here," he said refusing to look at me straight in the eyes.

"It's ok; I don't care where it is," I said aloof.

He turned around, and glared at me, "Why are you acting that way, first at school, the whole drive here and now, why are you giving me the cold shoulder?   ---And don't use that excuse that someone is going to see us, because look again no one is around for miles," he said agitated.

"I have my reasons."

"Which is?" He carefully studied my face while he waited for an answer. He then sighed. "You know what... I give up. I am getting tired of your childish ways," he walked away and let me standing there on my own.

Tears flowed down my face, I knew he was not human but I loved him anyways. In the still silence of my broken heart, I hated myself for doing this to him when I knew he cared for me. I took a deep breath and looked up at the twilight sky, which was slowly turning darker. Little diamond bright stars slowly showed up to this gloomy night. I closed my eyes and said to myself, *'I did it, he hates me now.'* My heart was torn, but it was for the best. This was the first step to begin planning my own funeral. A deep sense of relief overcame me, followed by one deep breath. I would be able to leave my sorry life behind when my mother died without hurting anyone, I thought to myself then I wiped the tears with the sleeve of my sweater and sneaked inside the cabin, but did not see anyone and headed to my room.   I had started to unpack, when I heard a knock on the door.

Emma announced herself and poked her head in, "hi, can we talk?"

"Sure, come on in," I placed the clothes on the bed.

"Hmm, it's about Victor."

I took a deep breath.

"I saw him kind of down and I asked him, but he didn't want to say ---are you guys having problems?"

I fidgeted with my hands, I was not sure if I should spill out my feelings to her, "Yes, I guess it's my fault, ---I'm sorry but he doesn't get it." I sat down on the edge of the bed.

"Amber he is my brother and I hate to see him that way, why don't' you tell me what's going on between you two, maybe I can help," she sat next to me.

I broke down and confided in Emma. I told her what my mother had planned for my future, and that Mr. and Mrs. Cromwell had agreed to be my guardian.

"So you see I have to end our relationship, before it gets more serious, we can't live under the same roof having feelings for each other," I said with a sad grimace.

"I understand what you're saying Amber, but things are different. I just wish I could tell you certain things, but I can't. —it is not my place," she held my hands and smiled, "but one thing I can tell you is that my brother is in love with you."

"Did he tell you that?"

"Yes, and I know that without you he will cease to exist, —that's kind of love cannot be turned off that easy," she paused and stared at me, "You do love him, don't you?"

I sighed, "Hmm to tell you the truth, I really don't know —I am so confused Emma."

"Well do you want him in your life?"

"Yes, I think so."

"Ok that's promising." She smiled, "while you figure out your feelings for him ---can you at least make this trip enjoyable for him, please? Remember we came to have fun."

"I'll try, Emma."

"Uhm... are you hungry?"

"No I'm good." I answered.

She sighed in relief, "Great because we didn't stop at the store for food, and the pantry is empty. But I'll promise I'll go early to get you something."

"It's ok," I lied hoping she would not hear my stomach growl.

She left and closed the door.

I turned on the TV and finished putting the clothes in the drawers of the dresser.

Later I found a candy bar inside my purse; my mom must have put it there for me, I thought and smiled, *'yeah mom!'* I said to myself before unwrapping slowly the candy bar. I looked out the window while I enjoyed every bite of the creamy chocolate.

It was still snowing. The snow had slowly piled up on the corners of the window, the cars parked outside covered in a white blanket of powder fresh snow. I saw Emma and Max quietly going for a walk while holding hands in the moonlit night. I saw them heading to the woods, then suddenly I could not see them anymore, I had lost them in the dark shadows casted by the tall pine trees. I wished that would be Victor and me taking a long walk in the privacy of the dark woods with only the moonlight to guide us, but that will never be us, thanks to my mother. I sighed and walked away from the window. I turned off the lights and slid under the covers, and cried myself to sleep.

Emma came to my room in the morning. She softly knocked on the door before she carefully poked her head in, as if she was afraid she was going to wake me up, but I was already up getting dressed, I was almost done putting on my boots.
I could see Victor standing behind her.
I smiled and said, "good morning" I zipped up the other boot.
"I am going to drive you to the store to buy the groceries, are you ready?" He asked.
I turned to look at Emma.
"I'm going too," Emma winked at me.
"Uhmm sure, I'm finished," I grabbed my jacket from the chair.
We went to the nearby store about ten miles away. Victor did not talk, he still seemed a bit upset, but Emma did all the talking for us.
At the grocery store I got a few things; Emma bought random stuff, more junk food than anything else.
We returned to the cabin with a few bags.
Emma put the groceries up and left us alone in the kitchen.
"Victor, can I talk to you?" I said humbly hoping that he would agree, and if he did not at least I could tell Emma I tried to be nice.
He scoffed, "Are you sure no one is watching us?" He said with sarcasm.
"Come on, I was going to call it truce."
"Truce, huh?"
"Yes, I'm sorry, really I am."
He stared deeply into my eyes, and then a smile suddenly appeared on his face when he saw that I was being truthful.
Max interrupted, "hey guys are you coming? We are going snowboarding."
"Sure. I'm in…" Then Victor turned to me, Are you coming?"

"I don't even know how to ski," I felt my face blush.

"I'll teach you, come on lets go it will be fun," Victor smiled.

I grinned, "Ok."

"Meet you guys in the car," Max said.

Victor nodded.

We reached the ski resort. We went to rent our gear. Max and Emma left to go up on the lift and let me alone with Victor.

Victor took me to the small hill to teach me, but I was not getting any good at it, I kept falling. My butt was getting sore from hitting the snow so many times. I tried it again, and I fell once more.

Victor laughed, and extended his arm to help me up again.

"I'm not a good student, aren't I?

He chuckled, "Can I be honest?"

"Sure," I rocked back and forth. I was having a hard time balancing.

"I think you suck," he grinned.

"Oh... thanks for being so honest," I laughed. "I know I do suck," I pouted.

He grabbed my waist to keep me from falling, "I know something you won't suck at, plus I think your butt needs a rest."

We helped me take off the skis and we walked back to the ski rental to return our gear, and we went snow tubing. I got this, there was no way I could screw this up, I thought with a smile on my face. Then finally, I was having a good time. The fun and excitement had helped me forget my heartache.

Victor seemed to be enjoying himself too. He raced me down the hill.

I reached the bottom of the hill before he did, "I beat you," I cheered.

"About time you did," Victor chuckled.

"Did you let me win?"

He grinned, "No."

I knew he did, but that was sweet of him.

He took me to the lodge to get warm up, but all I craved was a hot cocoa to warm up my bones, but he insisted that I went inside and warm up by the fireplace. He brought me a white mug with steaming hot chocolate topped with peppermint candy.

"You are not getting anything?" I blew on the chocolate to cool it down.

"No, I'll just have water," he said.

"Hmm... sorry I forgot."

He smiled and touched my cheeks, "Your cheeks are red."

"It's the cold wind, I can hardly feel them."

"So it was a good idea to get you out from the cold."

I smiled and sipped on the warm chocolate. The heat from the fireplace had reached all the right spots in my body.

His cell phone rang. Emma wanted us to meet them by the entrance they were ready to leave. I quickly finished with my drink and we headed to meet with Emma and Max. I slipped on the stairs but with his quick reflexes, he caught me on time.

"Careful, we need to take you back to your mom in one piece," he chuckled.

"Can I borrow your cell phone? I left mine in the room."

"Sure, are you going to call your mom?"

"Yeah just to see how she is."

He handed me the phone and I made a quick call to my mom. I told her a little about the excitement of the day, I promised to call her later to tell her more and we hanged up.

"Is she doing ok?"

"Yes. Here thanks," I handed him his cell phone.

I was cold but his smile warmed my heart.

I gazed at him and smiled.

He poked the tip of my nose with his index finger. "Let's go Rudolph."

Emma and Max were patiently waiting for us, and we drove back to the cabin.

It started to snow again, the little white flakes hitting the windows.

When we got out of the car, Emma and Max started throwing snowballs at each other, then they threw some at us and the snow fight started. We laughed so hard that we kept missing each other. We were just having lots of fun. I got Victor by mistake and he bent down to pick up some snow to throw it at me, I started running, not knowing I was too close to the edge of the stream, the edge was frozen and I slipped in the cold freezing water.

Victor jumped after me; he grabbed me and pulled me out and put me on the ground covered with snow.

We both were drenched from head to toe. I started shaking

immediately.

Emma and Max looked at me in shock.

Mrs. Cromwell had been watching us and ran to me to see if I was ok, and told Victor to take me inside immediately. Victor picked me up and carried me inside to my room. They all had followed us and were standing outside my room. I saw their worried expressions, but I could not understand why, it was not as if I had drowned.

When Victor put me down, Mrs. Cromwell suggested that I take the wet clothes off and take a hot shower immediately. Emma went to make me some tea and took Max with her.

Victor wrapped me in the blanket, "Are you ok?" He asked and helped me take my boots off.

"Yes, leave so I… I can get in the shower," I stuttered my teeth chattering

"Ok," he too looked worried.

"You go change too, you are wet," I smiled feeling ashamed for having been so clumsy.

"Don't worry about me," Victor said as Mrs. Cromwell ushered him out of the room and closed the door behind her.

I started undressing and dropped the cold wet clothes on the floor. I wrapped myself in one of the towels and turned on the hot water on the shower. I let it run hot to warm up the bathroom. Suddenly I felt hot air blowing out of the vents in the bathroom; they must have turned the heater. I smiled. I was about to step in the shower when I noticed a dark brown spider slowly crawling in the corner of the bathroom. I screamed and ran out of the bathroom to get something to smack the spider with, then the noise of the bedroom door busting open, made me jump.

Victor with his quick reactions had run inside my room like a flash and was standing next to me, "what's wrong?"

"There is a spider over there."

"A what?" He said calmly and raised his eyebrows.

"That big spider in the corner," I pointed.

"You are scared of that little thing?" He smiled.

"It's not little, look at its size," I said alarmed and frowned.

He shook his head, "So —what now? Are you expecting me to kill it?" He said amused.

"Well yeah, I was going to do it but since you're already here, you do it."

"Big baby," he turned off the shower, then grabbed a piece of paper and squished the spider, and flushed it down the toilet. "There, happy now?"

"Yes," I smiled and carefully looked inside the bathroom. I wanted to make sure that was the only bug the hot steam had disturbed.

He stood behind me.

"Amber!"

I turned and he looked stunned. I quickly turned around to look behind me, when I did not see anything I glanced back at him.

"What is it? You're scaring me."

He stepped back and sat down on the bed, "you lied to me." He did not sound happy.

"Me? What are you talking about?" I frowned confused.

He scoffed, "stop lying! You have a birthmark on your shoulder."

That's when I realized I was standing in front of him, half-naked with only a towel covering the middle part of me and Victor had seen my birthmark, which I had been secretly hiding from him all these weeks. I tightly closed my eyes. I knew I would get caught sooner or later, but not yet. "You are here for me right?" I pursed my lips, "You found me, didn't you?"

"How do you know all this?" He shook his head.

"I have seen you before Victor… in a dream," I confessed.

"You have seen me before?" He gave me an incredulous stare.

"Yes ---I had a dream before you guys moved in and when I saw you the first time I panicked, because I recognized you. I know you were looking for me, that you are here to get me, to claim me for the many times I have wished I was death."

With his eyebrows drawn together he asked, "I don't know how or why you know, but yes, I have been looking for the one with the precious stone name and a birthmark shaped like a butterfly on her back of her neck. But when my mom told me she saw it on your shoulder, I didn't believe her, I wanted to see it myself, but then you lied to me and I didn't know what to think, but now, that I know is you…"

"What are you going to do?" I asked frightened, I could hear the drumming beats of my heart beating faster.

"This changes everything, you are the one," he stood up and took a step toward me.

I immediately took a step back.

"You're scared."

"Yes, what do you expect?"

"Don't be," he approached me and looked at the birthmark closely. He then touched my face and kissed me in a way that he had never kissed me before.

I melted in his arms. I could feel the magic flowing in the air again. I wanted him more than I ever had. "Why are you kissing me like that now?" I opened my eyes after that wonderful kiss.

"Because, I can ---now that I found you, nothing is going to stop me. I can make you fall in love with me at anytime."

"You won't need to. ---I'm already in love with you," I divulged and took a deep breath. I finally told him.

"I thought so, but I need it to hear it from those beautiful lips," he kissed me again. He then slowly trailed kisses down my neck traveling down to my shoulder, returning back to my neck where he stopped and started sucking on one area. I could feel my eyes flipping. My body squirmed encouraging him. His body got rigid and he softly moaned.

I pulled away and looked at him, I saw his eyes turned black, his eyelids were different, the blood vessels around his eyes were more visible and a tone of dark blue almost black, making him look sinister almost like a monster. His beautiful face had changed to that of a scary creature, something evil and malevolent.

He looked down ashamed.

"What are you, Victor?" I asked scared after seeing his transformation come and fade away right before my own eyes.

"It's time that I tell you, but I think you already know ---I'm a vampire, Amber."

My eyes widened in shock, "You are a what?"

He frowned. "A vampire, you know I am not human."

"Yes, but…"

"What did you think I was?" He asked confused.

"I always thought you were the angel of death that had come for me… you know, like the grim reaper."

He chuckled, "You thought I was the grim reaper, really? Why?"

I explained my reasons for wishing to die. I told him how I hated the thought of losing someone I loved, and that when I learned about my mother's illness, I didn't want to be left alone in this world, so I swore that I would kill myself when she died.

"You want to die?" He shook his head, "I won't let you," he said vehemently.

"So you're not going to kill me?"

"No." He paused and then smiled, "at least not yet."

I gulped and covered my neck with both hands.

He laughed. "Stop! You are safe, just go take a shower. I'll be outside the door if you need me. Amber, we really need to talk."

I took a long hot shower while I tried to make sense of everything that had just happened. Here I was thinking all this time he was the reaper, and he is a real freaking vampire. I was amazed that explained a lot. I smiled and let the hot water warm my body.

Then I thought of Emma and Max, and Mr. and Mrs. Cromwell, they must be vampires too. My eyes widened when I realized I was alone in a house filled with vampires. Suddenly I felt a chill go down my back.

Then I thought of my poor mother thinking that she was saving me when in fact she was setting me up to be the main course. I shook my head and let out a little chuckle, before turning off the water.

CHAPTER 8

I put on my white wool sweater to keep me warm; black stretch pants, and my fluffy multicolored stripped socks. I stood in front of the mirror blow-drying my hair.

There was a knock on the door and I went to open.

Emma was holding a hot cup of tea, "here it is, that should warm you up." She said as the steam rose from the scalding tea.

"Thank you," I smiled softly and grabbed the hot cup with both hands praying that I would not sneeze.

"Uhm, Victor is outside waiting to talk to you; but he is worried, since you took a long time to get ready, ---he thinks you might be afraid of him, are you?" She asked.

"Sort of," I confessed. "Are you one too?"

"You mean a vampire?" She said casually.

"Yes," I replied.

"What do you think?" she smirked.

"I think so. You guys do some odd things sometimes."

"I guess you have been keeping a watchful eye on us," she grinned. "Yes we all are vampires."

I took a deep breath, "So… that makes me the only human in the house."

Filled with enthusiasm Emma told me that I was going to

become one of them, part of their family. But to me that only meant I had to die.

"Emma, will it hurt when I die?"

She grinned devilishly and did not answer me. "I will let Victor know, you are ready."

Her statement petrified me.

She saw the panic in my eyes and said, "—to talk, ready to talk. Geez, you are afraid of him," she smiled flashing her teeth and walked out of the room.

I paced around, I felt like an innocent caged animal waiting to get slaughter. I slowly sipped on the hot tea.

Victor knocked on the door and walked in. "Are you warm now?"

"Yes. Thank you."

"Would you like to sit down?" Victor looked nervous.

I sat on the bed and rested my back against the headboard. I continued to take small sips of the tea, until I finished.

Victor sat by the end of the bed, "is it ok if I sit next to you?"

"Uhm --sure," I said hesitantly, I did not know if he just needed to have a quick access to my neck.

He took the empty cup away from me and set it on the nightstand, "Amber is there anything that you would like to ask me?"

I thought for a moment, I had so many questions for him, he will be sorry he asked. I cleared my throat, "If you are not the angel of death, why exactly are you looking for me?"

"I have been looking all these years for that eternal love, someone to be my companion." He gently touched my hand. "And I have found her; and I want you as my bride."

"Me?" I asked surprised.

"Yes."

"Do I have an option here?"

"Not really," he gave me a crocked smile.

"So is that what Emma meant when she said I'll be one of you guys?"

"Yes, you will be one of us."

"I see," I took a deep breath and pondered, "I asked you if you were going to kill me and you said not yet, --so you weren't kidding?"

"No, I'll eventually need to suck the blood from your body to convert you and make you mine."

I was filled with awe from this significant moment. I was finally learning the truth about him and I would have a gratifying feeling, if it was not for the fact he was a vampire. Learning that vampires did exist was crazy and mind blogging, but the idea that I had confessed my love to a vampire was even more crazy and the worst part was that I contemplated becoming his.

"Will it hurt?" I asked.

"Does that mean you accept?

"I don't know Victor, I am confused. ---it's just too much for me to take in all at once." I had problems putting my words together, "uh… it's not easy for me ---or for anyone to find out they are in love with a dead person."

He smiled at my comment, "but it was ok for you when I was the grim reaper?" I don't get you Amber, I am the same Victor you met, —yes I am dead but I still have feelings," Victor said and continued, "feelings that won't go away. You belong with me. Our souls are connected. Our love will live forever and ever."

"Victor, but…"

"But what?" He leaned closer and kissed me, "Don't you love me?" He said in between kisses.

My body slid down from the sitting position, as if I was melting under him, he held himself up trying not to lay on top of me, his both arms erect on each side of me, I wrapped my arms around his neck and tried to pull him closer to me, but it was impossible, he was rigid and strong.

He continued kissing me in a very passionate way.

"Yes, I do, ---I do love you," I gasped for air and kissed him again, I craved more of his attention.

He stopped and moved back to where he was sitting a few minutes before and restrained himself from continuing further.

I lifted myself and scooted back to where I was sitting, and controlled my sexual impulses, just like a respectable young lady should, but in reality I was struggling with my inner self.

"Amber, if you love me it shouldn't matter what I am, right?"

I sighed. "No but…" I ran my fingers through my hair, "uhmm, I need more time."

"More time?"

"Yes, I have to think this through, you want me to leave my

mom, and I can't —she needs me."

"Baby, it won't happen right away. I have to wait until you are older. I made a promise," he smiled and continued saying, "I was surprised to find out how old you were. I was expecting my soul mate to be older than sixteen, that way I could do the transformation right away," he closed his eyes reminiscing. "I know it hasn't been even a month, but for me it has been an eternity, and suddenly the age was not a problem I could wait a little bit longer if I had to," a smile appeared on his face. "I remember what you wore that day, the look on your face when you first saw me. Your rosy cheeks couldn't hide your fear, those eyes that felt like a wooden stake driven into my heart. The smell of your sweet innocent scent when I walked down stairs it was intoxicating. Then I heard the sound of your voice coming out of those moist pink warm lips and the delicate soft touch of your hands, I was lost. I knew I had found you, after that first day you got me even if you were not my soul mate, but now, I am sure you are," he opened his eyes and stared at me,

Finally, he was telling me what I always suspected, what I wanted to hear. I smiled, and glanced down breaking his hypnotic stare. Then, I gently squeezed his hand.

He chuckled, "I have to admit, I was a little skeptical at some point, I wasn't sure that you were the one, but what I was feeling was real and I didn't care. I had never felt like that before, and when I hugged you and held you in my arms comforting your sorrow ---I didn't want to let go." He raised my chin our eyes met once more and he continued, "I was ready to make you mine that day," he paused and gave me a wicked smile, "you were this close to dying."

I let out a short nervous laugh. I felt my heart beating faster and I took a deep breath, "So you've loved me since the first day you saw me?"

"Yes, ---and you sure played hard to get," he stared at me with his hazel marbleized eyes.

"I was scared of you, I didn't know what to make of my dream, but now it all makes sense," I snickered, "But boy was I wrong. At first I thought I had a crush on the angel of death, but it wasn't a crush, what I was feeling was real."

He grabbed my hand and kissed it as I expressed my love for him.

"I'm sorry for the times I acted indifferent, I didn't mean to hurt you. Is just that I am scare, ---scare of loving someone and then they leave me, like my mom is planning on doing." My eyes immediately welled up and a few tears slowly ran down my cheek.

He gently wiped off the tears and kissed my cheeks, "Amber I want you to share eternity with me. I promise to love you forever, I will never leave you."

"Would you wait for me?"

"Yes, I will... I have waited for more than a century to find my soul mate —so what is an extra two years?" He smiled.

I giggled, "How old are you?"

"My real age? You don't want to know," he laughed.

"Yes I do, I want to know everything about you."

He held my hand and looked at me straight in the eyes, "I have been on this earth for One hundred and fifty years."

My eyes widened when I heard how old he was, but I did not care, he sure did not look that old. He continued to tell me everything about him and his past. He made himself comfortable on the bed, "I was born in Spain in eighteen fifty-nine, I had a sister named Ana, --she was only a year older than I was. She was engaged to be married to an older man, but she killed herself the night of her wedding; she was in love with someone else. My father also had arranged for me to get married to a fifteen year old girl from another wealthy family, who I detested, I did not love her, and neither did she love me. Back then you would have been of legal age to marry me, and I wouldn't be in this predicament," he chuckled.

I listened attentively to his life story, I held on tight to his hand, his cold fingers intertwined with mine.

He continued with the story, "So after my sister's death, my mother did not support my father on his decision and she and I decided to escape to Paris a few weeks before my arranged marriage would take place. I was a month shy from turning eighteen when a clan of vampires that were terrifying the city of Paris attacked me. I was left to die in a ditch. I was somewhere in between life and death when one of the vampires returned for me, —to finish me off. I could hear my heart slowly taking its last beat, until it stopped pounding. I woke up weak and hungry, —he made me drink some of his blood to nourish me, and gave me a second chance. I didn't have a heart beat but I was alive," he stared at the wall in silence, he seemed to be a million miles away, transported to another era, then he lowered his gaze and returned his eyes to me, "...and that's how I became what I'm today, —a vicious monster."

"You are not monster."

"You have seen me when I get near you and smell your blood, I become a monster. I want to bite you and drain the last drop of blood from your body."

"Don't say that... you scare me."

"Sorry, but that's the truth." His seductive smile twisted on the corners of his mouth.

"You never answered me, is it going to hurt?" I watched his expression. I studied his face, my eyes tracing his perfect face and beautiful lips.

"Do you want to be like me?" He had a grimace on his face.

I took a deep breath, "maybe, if I'm with you." I was tempted to close my eyes, but kept them open. I was ready for him, to be his was going to worth the pain.

"It will hurt a little of course, but you will lose consciousness very quick and I'll be able to finish you off without you suffering."

I tried not to shake. I could hear the sound of my heartbeat roaring in my ears, "What happens then?"

"You'll wake up, drink my blood for nourishment and become like me. I'll be your maker."

I gulped.

There was a knock on the door, Emma walked in and interrupted us, "Victor, we are leaving, are you coming?"

"No, I'll skip dinner tonight," Victor answered.

"Ok," Emma smiled and left.

I looked at the time; it was already ten at night. I glanced at him, "Is that were you guys go at night?"

He smiled, "Yes, we go hunt."

I said alarmed, "People?"

He snickered, "No, animals. The best ones are in the woods."

I was in awe, I thought that was what vampires did, —I guess I was wrong. Then with my lips parted slight, I asked intrigued, "You don't kill people then?" I wondered about his diet.

"We try not to. It's too much work trying to dispose of their bodies, killing an animal is way easier."

"So normally you wouldn't kill people for their blood?"

"No, except on a special occasion like it will be on your case, or if we are provoked," he smiled.

He touched my face tenderly, "Don't be scared," he smiled, "I can hear your heartbeat from here."

I grinned, "Sorry."

"Don't be," he leaned closer and softly pressed his soft velvety lips against mine. His tender kisses felt like butterflies wings caressing my lips.

I closed my eyes as I felt his lips teasing me and awaking that inner desire I felt before. I was hungry for more I wanted him to devour me the way he had done earlier but he continued to kiss me the same tender way. His butterfly kisses were a torture for me; I whimpered once more feeling brazen.

"Victor," I said his name my lips partly opened waiting for a more passionate kiss from him.

Then he slowly moved away, pressed his cheek against mine, and whispered in my ear, "yes, my love."

My hands roved over his back and I awoke a deep elation in him, his soft kisses were hungrier, his lips traced my neck, his magnificent body shuddered, but he pushed away.

"Don't stop." I tried to hold on to him, and wrapped my arms around his neck.

Victor wiggled his way free from my grasp and sat on the corner of the bed, "I have to. You still have not given me a straight answer. Do you want to be my bride?"

"I don't know what to say." I bit my lips.

"A 'yes' would be nice," he grinned.

I crawled my way to him on top the bed, and kneeled in front of him, "Victor, kiss me," I wanted to get lost in his arms. I wanted to feel that desire again.

"No, not until you give me your answer."

"It's not so easy, I want to say yes, I really do, but I'm scared."

"I know it may sound scary, but don't be, we will be together forever —just say, yes."

I had a sensation of flutter in my belly, "…but."

"But nothing," he held my hands, "I have waited too long for this moment. —I'm promising you eternal life, one that you will share with me," he spoke tenderly.

"But what if I am not your soul mate, and you find her one

day, --then you will leave me."

He giggled, "No silly, you are her," he said with conviction. "You are my soul mate, someone told me so."

"Huh?" I looked at him confused.

He smiled, "when I gave up hope of finding a mate, Emma took me to see Kaciba, an elder African vampire. He has the power of seeing things, he told me I would find love, to look for you, my soul mate. --he described the girl I was to fall in love, the one that would be my bride, a girl with the precious stone name and the butterfly birthmark on the back of her neck," he snickered, "he even told me in what city and street to find her. And after meeting you, and feeling the way I did and still do, I don't think he was wrong." His face filled with elation and his eyes glittered with an inner light.

I had already made up my mind, I knew what I wanted, but I decided to continue to give him a hard time, and keep him wondering a little bit longer. I grinned deviously inside my head. "Why look for love, isn't it supposed to find you?"

"Yes but sometimes there are exceptions, and you have to look for it, that's why I came to find you," he smiled. "I had a lot of encouragement, especially from Emma. She wants me to be happy like she is."

His eyes met mine and he held my hands tight.

"Emma also searched for her love and she found him," he said.

"Do you mean Max?"

"Yes, did you know she made him?"

"No," I shook my head.

"Yeah, we were living in New York; he was a struggling musician, Maximilian Black. She befriended him and he fell in love with her. After one of his auditions, he was in a motorcycle accident; he was in the hospital dying. Emma had also developed feelings for him and did not want to lose him, and that day at the hospital she bit him, Aubrey and I had to help her with his body, we brought him back to our house and she slit her wrist and made him drink her blood nurturing him back to life."

"And he is not mad that she killed him?" I asked.

"He was going to die, and besides he loves her, they are inseparable, there is nothing he wouldn't do for her, and that's what I want, someone to make me laugh, to hold in my arms, and to love forever."

"Did Emma tell you about my mom's plans for me?"

"No, Aubrey did... is that why you were treating me so cold earlier?"

"Yes. ---I didn't want to be your sister."

He smiled, "Silly, even if Aubrey and Estella would adopt you legally, you wouldn't be my sister. Remember, I'm not Aubrey's son or Estella's."

I hugged him feeling relieved from the huge burden my mother had placed on me, "So, they didn't adopt you?"

"No, vampires don't adopt their kids, —they just invite them to be in their family," he snickered, "I found Aubrey and Estella, and they have been my family ever since. We all use his last name just for appearance."

"Are they also from the nineteenth century?"

"Yes, mid-eighteen hundreds."

"Wow, so it's like in the movies, vampires don't age at all."

He smiled, "But don't belief everything you read or see on TV about us, most of it is just Hollywood glamour."

I chuckled and snuggled closer to him. I looked up, "How about Emma, same century?"

"Oh Emma ---I found her crying in an alley in Paris. She was a teenage courtesan. Her father was exploiting her, and had traded her to a benefactor, a noble married man. She did not want to continue living that life and she was ready to kill herself, and end it. I told her what I was and that I could help her escape that life, and she agreed."

"You made her for you?"

"Uhm... no, I didn't. I took her to meet Aubrey, once Estella saw her she wanted her as her daughter, she already had a son, me."

"So you didn't kill her?"

He narrowed his eyes, and with a pinched expression on his face, he was ready to answer me, when my cell phone rang interrupting him.

My mother called to check up on me. I spoke to her briefly, while Victor lay down on the bed and observed my every move. I finished talking to her.

Victor rested on the bed with his hands behind his head, "Is she ok?"

"Yes, she is just lonely without me," I chuckled. I took the opportunity that he was laying down and snuggled back next to him. "So where were we?"

"I was telling you about Emma."

"Oh yes, Emma's story is sad, being exploited like that."

"Yeah, back then everything was different, that was very common."

"So you are from Spain and she is from France, right? So, what happened to her dad?"

"We couldn't stay in Paris, so we moved to around from city to city and she never saw him again."

"How about your mom?"

I moved my head to his chest and tried to listen for a heartbeat and there was none. He hugged me, and pressed me against his chest.

"My mother," he sighed, "Maria Cristina Cortes Sabatini, she was very beautiful, her parents were immigrants from Italy… when we left to Paris to hide, she got sick with the influenza and died. I was all alone in a strange country without a family. I never knew what happened to my father, and I didn't care. Then about fifty years ago, I went back to Spain, and saw his name on the family crypt."

"So your real name is Victor Cortes?" I asked amazed.

"Yes, ---its Victor Antonio Cortes Sabatini," he chuckled. "It has being a long time since I had said my full name."

"I like it." Then the wheels turned inside my head, "Did Aubrey wait to make Emma a vampire?"

"No, Emma was transformed the same day she agreed."

"But didn't you say she was a teenager?" I asked confused.

"Yes, she is eighteen ---or was eighteen."

I stared at his face, "What? She told me she was twenty two."

He chuckled, "She lied; sometimes I lie too and tell people I'm twenty one," he smiled.

"You're kidding."

"No. We can't always be moving around, so we stay a few years in some places, and of course we have to get older, so we change our appearance a little."

I smiled amused, "Will I be able to do that too?"

"Yes, of course…" he stopped and looked at me with a

delighted smile, "does that mean you agree?"

I cuddled up back in his arms, "hold me."

"You are not answering," he kissed the top of my head.

I lifted my head and pulled myself up, so that we could see eye to eye, our glance locked together. I gently touched his face and outlined his lips with my index finger.

He bit the tip of it.

"Ouch!" I exclaimed.

He smiled.

I looked at my finger he had drawn blood. I went to put it in my mouth.

He grabbed my hand, a drop of blood emerge from my finger, "Let me do that," he sucked the tip of my finger and he would not stop.

I was uncomfortable, "Ouch… don't... no more," I pulled my hand away.

He looked thrilled, "it's just a little taste, that didn't hurt," he grinned.

"Are you going to give me some sort of warning before you sacrifice me?"

"Is this one of your elusive ways of answering, yes?"

I smiled coyly, "Yes, I'll be your bride."

He flipped me over on my back, and jumped on top of me like a predator pinning down its prey. "Do you mean it?" he said jubilant and smiled from ear to ear.

My heard pounded feeling afraid, "yes, but don't scare me like this."

"Sorry," he got off me.

I sat up, "would you tell me before you do it. I want to be prepared."

"That wouldn't be fun. It would be like a lion ringing a dinner bell before pouncing on a zebra," he chuckled.

"Not funny."

"I got to tell Emma, you said yes," he said excited.

"Wait! Kiss me," I pulled him back into my arms.

He proceeded to give me more sweet, gentle, fluttering kisses, the ones that felt like butterfly kisses.

"Not like that ---like you did a while ago." I whispered softly.

"We have to wait, I get too excited and I won't be able to

control myself and I will kill you."

"But I am going to be your bride… you can kiss me," I persuaded him.

He gave in to me and kissed me passionately.

I was getting excited, and so was he, he dropped kisses down my neck, I could feel his teeth poking me lightly but didn't pierce my skin. My body got tense as I waited eagerly for him to bite me, I was ready, but nothing happened.

He looked at me, and licked his lips, as if he was savoring the flavor of my flesh. He was hungry, hungry for me. I could feel it, and it made me nervous.

"What's up with that serious face?" He asked and then tickled me.

"Stop it," I laughed.

There was a knock on the door again.

"Come in," I said.

This time it was Mrs. Cromwell. She held the door open and saw us on the bed.

"Victor what are you doing?" She raised her eyebrow.

"Playing with my food," he looked at me and laughed.

"Totally not funny," I shoved him.

Mrs. Cromwell laughed. "I'm glad to see you two getting along… hand me those wet clothes, so I can put them in the drier."

He picked up my clothes off the floor.

"The boots too," she said.

Victor walked to the door and handed her the clothes.

I saw him whisper in her ear.

She smiled, "Oh honey, I'm so happy for you," she touched his face in a motherly caring way.

He closed the door and leaned against it.

"Did you tell her?" I could feel my cheeks flushing.

"Yes," he smiled.

"I can't wait to get home," I grinned.

"Why?"

"So that I can tell my mom, —this is not the type of news you can tell over the phone," I chuckled.

His expression changed immediately, he had a grim set look on his face, "you can't."

"Why? She is my mom, she needs to know."

He sat next to me and stared at me with his piercing eyes, "what I told you today, is just between us, no one else can know."

"But you told your mom," I said with a sad grimace.

"It's our family secret, your mom is human."

"And so am I."

"But not for long, you are going to be one of us," he made the effort to sound reassuring.

"But Victor…" I protested.

"Shhh…" He silent me with a long drugging kiss.

I quickly immersed in his essence and the sweetness of his lips.

He gently released me, and steadily stared into my eyes, "You can't tell her or anyone else for that matter, promise me."

After a moment of reflection, I agreed. "Ok."

CHAPTER 9

Victor guarded me all night, he was the first thing I saw when I opened my eyes in the morning. He was sitting on the recliner chair by the door.

"Great! You are awake," Victor faced beamed with happiness.

I yawned and stretched, "yeah, you too."

"We don't sleep," he lamented.

"You don't?"

"No, we close our eyes but we are not asleep, just resting."

"I guess there is a lot of stuff that I need to learn about being a vampire, huh?"

"You are not one yet, plus you'll have two years to learn," he got up the chair, "Come on get ready. I'll take you to eat breakfast."

"Ok."

"Don't take too long," he left the room so that I could get ready.

I was alone with my thoughts, everything was so confusing and surreal, but the one thing I was certain of was that I loved him and one day I was going to be a vampire too. The thought of being a vampire made me smile; I would not have guessed that in a million years.

Today we were to head back home. I packed my duffle bag.

While I enjoyed being with Victor and I wished I could spend more time alone with him, I still missed my mother, she needed me more than ever. I met Victor downstairs in the living room Emma, Max and Aubrey were excited with the news and congratulated us.

Then Estella walked in, "I knew it was you, welcome to our family," she hugged me, "he is madly in love with you, but you know that, right?"

"Estella," Victor said embarrassed.

I smiled and winked at her.

"We'll be back shortly. I have to take Amber out to eat." Victor drove to the nearest town ant stopped at the first restaurant he saw so that I could eat breakfast.

"Victor, ---is it true about the wooden stake and coffins?"

He burst out laughing, "No to the coffin, the wooden stake is real, that's one way to kill us. It's unconventional but effective."

"So it's possible for you guys to die?" I questioned.

"Yes, --but it's almost impossible for someone to get close to our kind, we would be able to feel their intentions, ---unless…"

"Unless what?"

"The stabbing is self inflicted."

"But who would do that, from what you have told me, ---I think being a vampire is pretty cool."

"Shh… lower your voice," he looked around.

There was a woman sitting with her children on a nearby table and had turned to look at us then one her children distracted her.

"You think it's cool…" He whispered and continued with a grin, "do you know I have the ability to make you love me, to make you do what I want?"

"Get out of here… like mind control?"

"Yes."

I lowered the tone of my voice, "see --that is super cool, --I wish I had that."

He smiled, "finish eating, we need to get going. I don't want your mom to worry ---then she won't trust me with you again."

I chewed the last bite of the pancake and swallowed, and then I remembered my mother sudden change when she met Victor. I scoffed, "Did you use your powers on my mom?"

He lowered his head ashamed, "Yes, if I didn't she wasn't

going to let me date you at least not yet, ---I had to do something."

"I knew it... I knew there was something wrong with her."

"But why did you plant the idea on her head that your parents should be my legal guardians?"

"I didn't, Estella and Aubrey were taken by surprise too. Your mom came up with that one by herself," he grinned. "What I did was just get her to approve of me seeing you. She did admit before I persuaded her that she thought I was nice young man, only that she was concerned of the age difference and of your innocence and inexperience in the dating department, ---so I really didn't do much to change her mind. She likes me," he said proudly.

"She seems to trust you more than she does me," I said regretfully.

"Not really, she just likes the way she feels in our presence; it makes her feel fully charged and happy."

"That's why your parents took her out that evening?"

"Right, --- are you ready?" he raised his eyebrow and waited for my reply.

"Sure," I wiped my mouth with the napkin and placed it on the table.

We headed back to the lodge. Emma and Max were loading their car. Victor started doing the same. I brought my duffle bag downstairs.

Victor met me by the entrance. "My love, let me get that for you," he gave me the sweetest smile, his hazel eyes sparkled with joy.

Through the drive back, we held hands, although they were cold I did not care. Every time I would glance at him, and our eyes met, he would smile. At one point, he kissed my hand. He stared at me avidly. I wanted to put my arms around him, but I refrained.

Then after a while of flirting with each other, a spark lighted his fire and he could not resist and urgently captured my lips in an engulfing kiss, but then Aubrey cleared his throat, expressing disapproval and broke the spell.

Victor immediately pulled away and abruptly stared at Aubrey, who was looking at us through the rearview mirror, although Victor's reaction seemed antagonistic, he did not question Aubrey's judgment.

I ashamedly slouched in the seat and bit my bottom lip.

Aubrey and Estella did not say anything, but I knew we had done something inappropriate. Although, they were cold-blooded vampires, they still behave like human parents.

Victor was relaxed and quiet. The rest of the way, we only held hands, but I had to put my mittens on after awhile when I could not resist the coldness of his hand.

We made it back home. My mother's car was parked outside on the driveway.

Victor and Aubrey walked me to the front door of my house, as if I needed to be escorted to cross the street.

My mother heard us coming and opened the door. She did not look the same way, as I had left her; she looked pasty white, and frail. I was a little shocked to see her that way, since she had told me that she was feeling good.

"Thank you for bringing her back home," My mother said to Aubrey, with a note of relief.

"She was a delight to be with. We had fun," Aubrey commented with a smile.

"Good. I am sure she is going to tell me all about it."

"Thank you Mr. Cromwell for everything. I'll see you later Victor." I saw the pain and anxiety in his eyes, he was feeling the same I was. I did not want to let him go.

"Yes, later," he said with a sad smile.

I closed the door.

My mother anxiously pulled me to the living room. "Come on tell me. How was it?"

"Good."

I told her every that we did, and how bad I was at skiing. I was making her laugh. I wished I could tell her the best part of this trip, that I had confessed my love to Victor and that he was in love with me too. That Victor in a few years was going to be her son in law and that he was a real vampire, but I could not; I had made a promise to Victor.

My mother was glad that everything had gone well with the Cromwells.

I went to my room to get my stuff ready for school on Monday.

I closed the door and reached for the light switch. Someone held my hand over the switch, and covered my mouth.

"Shh... it's only me," Victor turned on the light.

I locked the door, "What are you doing here? I whispered.

He grinned, "I missed you already... I wanted to give you a goodnight kiss."

"You miss me?" I wrapped my arms around his neck.

"Yes... do you know how much I love you?" He continued to whisper, and held me by the waist.

"I think I have an idea," I smiled, and whispered to him in ear, "Kiss me."

"Just a little one, I don't want to get carried away, like I did in the car, I was a little out of line --sorry."

"It wasn't just you --my blood starts to boil when you touch me," I grinned, "I liked it. It was wonderful," I admitted.

"I know, but we shouldn't, I have to wait until you are older," he tilted his head down, "Try to restrain yourself, missy," he smiled impishly.

I lowered my arms and put them behind my back, crossing my wrist. "Is that better?"

"Yes," he gently held my face and outlined my lips with soft, sweet delicious kisses, the ones that felt like butterfly kisses.

I had my eyes closed, I felt like a feather floating on air.

"Mmm," he uttered, "goodnight."

I opened my eyes, "goodnight."

He walked slowly to the window.

"Victor," I said his name softly, I did not want my mother to hear me.

He turned around, "Yes Amber?" He seemed dismal.

"I love you," I uttered.

His somber expression turned into a beautiful smile, "come here."

I pranced to his side.

"Can you say it again?" He held me in his arms.

I looked at him straight into his hypnotic eyes, "I love you Victor," I proclaimed.

A single drop of blood rolled down his face.

I saw him bleeding through his eyes, but then I recognized what it was, "is that a tear?" I asked amazed and gently stroke his face in a loving manner.

He wiped it off, "I'm sorry, it's just that those words mean a lot to me, especially coming from you."

I Smiled. "Well get ready to hear it a lot, because that's how I really feel ---just promise me you won't ever leave me."

"I won't, ---I love you too much Amber, I don't know what I would do if I lost you."

"Don't worry, it's like you said --you found what you were looking for."

"Do you mind if I stay a little bit longer, I'll promise not to make any noise?"

"Aubrey is not going to like it."

"He just wants me to take it slow with you, that's all."

"Sounds like my mom," I chuckled.

Victor stayed while I picked out my clothes for the next day. I went to the restroom to change to my flannel pajamas.

He was sitting on the edge of my bed when I came out. He snickered, "Don't you look sexy," he said with sarcasm.

"Oh... hush, it's a cold night."

He chuckled, "I guess is time for me to go."

"Yes, sir."

"Now who is trying to be funny?"

"My mom thought me to call my elders sir or ma'am as a form of respect," I said with a smug on my face.

He wrapped his arms around my waist. "And you young lady are in love with this old vampire."

"I know --how sick is that?" I grinned.

"That is very sick," he softly dropped kisses all over my neck, he proceeded to my ear and nibbled on it, "what wouldn't I give to make you mine right now," he whispered.

"I dare you," I taunted him.

He raised his eyebrows and tilted his head to the side. "Really? Are you tempting me?" His expression was grave.

My body got tense, but I challenged him, "Do it!"

He turned around and sat on the edge of the window, "You are one brave little girl, ---close your window."

"I am not a little girl," I said in a chiding tone.

"Do what I tell you and don't entice me that way again, --that was cruel," he smiled faintly and jumped down with such ease.

Next morning, he waited for me outside on the porch to take

me to school.

I kissed my mother goodbye, but before closing the door she said, "Victor, take care of my precious baby."

"I always do, you don't need to ask me Mrs. Ross."

"Bye mom, have a good day."

"You two behave," she smiled.

During the school day, Brad approached me when I was alone grabbing a notebook from my locker.

"Get away from me," I slammed the door to my locker.

He grabbed my arm, "do you think you are hot stuff because you are going out with that freak?"

"Let go of her," Victor had appeared from nowhere.

Brad turned to look at him, "you and me after school," Brad told Victor. Brad's arm was still on a sling.

Victor pointed at Brad's arm, "What are you going to do? That wouldn't be a fair fight."

"You just meet me outside," Brad said in a menacing way.

Victor scoffed, "if you are so pumped up, why not now?" Victor replied.

"I'll see you after school," Brad walked away with his solidly built buddies.

"Are you ok?"

"Yes... Victor." I place my hand on his chest. "Don't meet him, don't give him the pleasure, they are going to jump you."

He snickered, "you don't think I can take them... remember who you are talking to."

I knew he wanted to defend my honor, but I did not want him to get in trouble because of me.

At the end of the school day, Victor waited for me outside the school as usual. I did not see Brad only his brawny friends, who were standing outside staring at us.

Victor opened the passenger car door and held it open for me.

"Hey, I guess Brad chickened out," I said and got in the car.

"He won't bother you anymore." He slammed the door.

I waited for him to get in the car, "Victor, what did you do?"

He raised his left eyebrow and gave me a devious look, "Nothing."

But of course I did not believe him, especially now that I knew what he was.

When he took me home, we found the front door wide open. Victor protectively went ahead of me to look. Estella and Emma were with my mom sitting on the couch. My mother was leaning back, forcing herself to breathe.

Emma rushed to Victor and me, "she called us. She is not doing good Amber. She needs to get to the hospital."

I rushed to her side, "mom, what's wrong?"

"Baby, I am not feeling good, ---I thought it was something that was going to pass," she heaved.

"Mom lets go, I'll call your doctor to let him know."

"I already did; he wants me to go right away."

"Ok then, ---what are you waiting for?"

"You," Emma answered with a twist of the mouth. "She didn't want to go until you got home."

"Oh, mom," I said miserably.

Victor helped me get her to the car, but my mother took slow uneven steps. I turned to look at Victor, and without saying a word to him —he understood what I wanted. Victor scooped her up and put her in the car.

At the hospital, the doctor prepared me for the worst. This was it. The rest of the week I spent it at the hospital with her, the hospital rather became my home.

Victor missed school too; as usual, he was by my side offering me his shoulder to cry on, showing me his love and support.

I was desperate. I did not want her to die, but the doctors had already given up; it was matter of days or hours.

Mrs. Cromwell came to visit, and brought my mother her briefcase from work. I saw my mother pull out an envelope from there and hand it to her. Mrs. Cromwell left immediately, smiling at me on her way out.

"Why didn't you ask me to bring it?" I asked my mother.

"I needed to give her something from here,"

"What was in that envelope?"

"Don't ask?"

"Huh," I mumbled in disapproval.

Later, I met with Victor outside the hospital. We went for a short walk, I wanted to ask him for a miracle, and I did, I wanted my mother to live forever. I asked Victor to bite my mother and give her a second chance.

My request seemed to catch him by surprise, because he hesitated and then said in a dismal tone, "I can't Amber."

"What do you mean you can't, don't you love me? Don't you want to see me happy?"

"You know I would do anything for you, --but I can't do that. Her body is already deteriorating, certain types of blood can make us sick, even kill us."

I loss control and raised my voice, "What are you saying that my mother blood can kill you… that you will not give her a second chance?" I held back what I thought were angry tears, but they were tears of defeat.

"Shh…" He looked around for any spectators, "Amber, please understand," he said with a sense of guilt.

My voice cracked, "well I don't, the time I need you the most you turn your back on me," I clenched my fists, and stomped back in to the hospital, while a waterfall of tears cascaded down my face, I had lost all hope.

"Amber, wait!" Victor hollered.

He caught up with me, "Wait, --Amber I love you, never doubt it"

"Prove it then," I sobbed.

"Amber please, --we have done a lot to make her feel comfortable doesn't that count?"

"No. I need her with me, and if you really love me you would do it." I cried and wiped the tears from my face with rage.

Victor stood silent averse to my idea.

I could not stop the tears they were rolling down uncontrollably. My heart was bleeding by his lack of feelings, "It's over… I take it back… I don't want to be your bride, --I lied I don't love you Victor!" I shouted with anger.

"Amber, you can't be serious," he stared at me in horror.

"I don't want to see you again Victor," I felt my heart ripped into pieces.

"You are just upset now, you don't mean it. You do love me, you said so."

"I lied, --don't talk to me again, I can only love someone that loves me back, and you obviously don't. My mother is the only family that I have, and she loves me and I love her," I closed my eyes, the pain I was feeling was unbearable, "--and I will be with her." I mumbled. Suddenly I found peace and comfort in my words. I was going to be with my mother. Then the last teardrop rolled down my cheek, I had to be strong if I was to let him go. I turned around and walked toward the entrance, I felt a cold breeze; it gave me shivers, then the automatic glass door of the hospital opened. Victor did not follow me.

The next two days I stayed with my mother, there was no way I was going to leave her alone, I did not care if I failed tenth grade. She looked worst. I brushed my mother's brittle hair; big chunks of it were falling off. My mother was having trouble breathing. She could not talk much.

The doctor called me outside the room to speak to me. He wanted me to make sure I had everything in order for her passing away, especially what I was going to do when she was gone; he called in a social worker, who took me to her office downstairs. That really made me angry, that the City was already thinking where to place me. I was rude and ill tempered to the social worker, and stomped out of her office.

When I was heading back upstairs to my mother's room, I saw Victor and Mr. Cromwell exiting the elevator. "What are you doing here? I told you I didn't want to see you anymore." I yelled at him.

"Amber calm down, we just went to visit your mother," Mr. Cromwell said.

I was still feeling indignant from the meeting with the social worker, "I don't care. He knows I don't want him here," I said brusquely.

I noticed Victor's eyes filled with pain, but I did not care; I was hurting more, I had lost him, and I was losing my mother.

Victor lowered his head, and indignantly walked out of the hospital without saying a word to me.

"We are leaving Amber, sorry to have upset you with our visit," Mr. Cromwell said.

I went upstairs to my mother's room. When I opened the door, I startled her. She was sealing an envelope, her hands were trembling, and she looked a little jittery.

"You just missed Victor, he seemed withdrawn. Is

everything ok with you and him?" She inquired doubtfully.

"I don't want to talk about it mom."

"Ok," she wrote my name on the envelope. "This is for you, open it when I am gone; I need to let you know that I..." She started coughing uncontrollably.

I panicked, "mom," I cried and ran to her side. I gave her the last few drops of water that were in the empty pitcher, but it was enough for her clear her throat.

When she was able to talk again she continued, "Ok I'll put it with the rest of the documents that you are going to need, ----I am leaving you my life savings, which is not much, —but it can help you out," she took deep breaths between words. "Amber ---do me a favor?"

"Anything mom," I was devastated. If this were the way, it felt when you were losing someone. I would rather be death.

"I want you to talk to Victor; he told me you guys had a misunderstanding."

"No!" I said adamantly, "I will do anything but that."

"You are so stubborn," she coughed. "Ok, can you get me some more ice and water, please?"

"Sure mom," I managed to give her a smile, but hiding behind this mask was fear, anger and grief caused by all the misfortune I was experiencing at once.

"Come here," she hugged me tight, and kissed my cheek.

I did not want her to see me cry, I could not do this to her, and I was strong and did not cry, "It's only a pitcher with ice and water," I said being muffled by her constricting hug.

She chuckled. "I love you." She said softly and blew me a kiss.

"I love you too, I'll be right back."

When I returned the doctors were leaving her room and had pronounced her dead, I dropped the pitcher on the tiled floor. A quick trip to the ice machine was long enough for me to miss her last breath. That was the last time I spoke to my mother.

CHAPTER 10

I saw Victor at my mother's funeral paying his last respect. He was not alone he was with his vampire family. He kept his distance and did not say a word to me, which it hurt me even more.

A couple of days had passed since my mother's funeral. I was alone in the empty and quiet house. I had started packing my stuff. I needed to turn the house over to the owner.
Then the doorbell rang.
It was Mrs. Cromwell, "Hi Amber, may I come in?"
"Sure," I stepped aside to let her in.
"How are you holding up?"
"I am just dealing with it the best I can."
"I know this is probably not a good time, but we are leaving and I need to return this to you." She handed me an envelope. "Aubrey and I are going to negate on the agreement we had with your mother, those are the papers. We won't ask for your custody… you understand why?"
Although I did understand, hearing their decision disappointed me. My shoulders drooped. "Yes, I do," I said with empathy.
She stared deep in my eyes, "Victor is devastated… have you changed your mind?"

"No," I said dejectedly.

"Do you know where you are going?"

With a grimace I said, "I don't know for sure. I spoke to Father Patrick and he thinks I can help the nuns at the orphanage," My voice sounded slightly brittle.

"I see... well Amber it was very nice to meet you," she said in her usual calm voice.

"You too, Mrs. Cromwell," I hugged her.

"Have a nice life," she smiled pleasantly and she left.

I looked out the window, and stared at the big house, a 'for sale' sign was out on the front lawn of the property. I felt a stabbing pain in my chest when I noticed that Victor's car was already gone. Then with tears in my eyes, I saw Mr. and Mrs. Cromwell drive off without turning back, just as if I had never existed.

I felt like I had been living a bad dream that had gone horribly wrong and I just wanted to wake up from this nightmare to the way it was before, but that was never going to happen, I was completely alone with not a friend in the world. The idea of dying crossed my mind several times. I did not want to live anymore. I did not have a future and nothing to look forward. The thought of joining my mother in heaven made me feel happy. I finished packing what I was taking with me. The rest Father Patrick said that they could sell it at the church annual garage sale that was coming soon, and the other stuff I donated them.

When I was packing the stuff in the kitchen, I accidentally broke a glass; I grabbed the dull end of one of the pieces. I thought of my way out, —I was expecting that it would be easier but I was lacking courage, I then took a deep breath and pressed the sharp edge against my wrist making a small incision. I panicked when I saw all the blood gushing out. I wrapped it with the kitchen towel. The towel was getting soaked with blood. I did not know what to do. I did not have Victor anymore to help me. I put pressure on it, but I was feeling woozy, and I blacked out.

I woke up in the hospital bed.

"I am glad you are awake," Father Patrick said.

"What happened?" I said frailly.

"You lost a lot of blood... you should had been more careful."

I remember the blood soaked towel, and immediately looked at my wrist wrapped in white bandage.

Father Patrick continued, "---if it had not had been for your friend, you would have bled to death."

"My friend?"

"Yes, the young man that lives across the street from you."

"Victor? Is he here?"

"No, he dropped you at the hospital and called me to let me know that you needed help; once I got here he left."

"Oh," I said disappointed.

In the morning, I was released from the hospital, no one questioned my injury, I was free to go but under Father Patrick's supervision. I never confessed to Father Patrick my secret. To him it all had been a clumsy accident. I was ashamed I could not admit that I had tried to end my life.

Father Patrick had moved my personal belonging to the orphanage already. That big strange place was going to be my new home. Father Patrick parked his white minivan by the curb outside the orphanage run by nuns. An old red brick building in the middle of historic downtown; a tall black iron bar fence surrounded it; the white faded paint of the window frames were more noticeable by the red bricks of the building.

Sister Delia came to the front gate to greet me. She was dressed in her black habit clothes. She did not look too old, but she did appear strict. The natural complexion of her oily face shined in the cold sunny day. She had slightly wrinkles on the side of her mouth when she smiled, "you must be Amber," Sister Delia said.

"Yes ma'am."

"Call me Sister Delia," she said to me. She then addressed Father Patrick. "Thank you Father Patrick, I'll take it from here."

"Amber, you are in good hands, I'll keep in touch," Father Patrick smiled.

I hugged him. "Thank you Father."

"Come on, Amber. I'll take you to your room," Sister Delia put her arms around me. She took me to my room on the second floor. The old, pine wooden floors creaked as we walked. Then she took me to tour the orphanage, to meet the other nuns, and the orphans that I was to help with. There were about fifteen orphan kids all of different ages, but mostly young, the oldest one could not have been more than ten years old.

I settled in my room. I looked out the window. It was snowing outside. The snow was accumulating outside on the windowsill. It reminded me of the lodge of that blissful night with Victor.

Sister Delia knocked on the door and told me to turn off the lights. They had their schedule, and it was time for me to turn in.

I did what she said, although I had a restless night and could not sleep much.

In the morning, Sister Delia came for me and took me to the kitchen so that I could help with the breakfast for the little ones, and they became my new family.

After the holidays, I returned to school. I had to make up for all the time I lost.

I went back to my old school. My arrangement with the nuns was to help with the orphans in the evenings, weekends and during the summer vacation. I was not going to be placed on adoption as my mother feared when she was alive. In return, the nuns gave me a place to stay and food on my plate, which it was not a bad deal, —the little ones helped me ease the pain from losing my mother and Victor.

There was no more gossiping in the school hallways, everyone was ignoring me. I was invisible, and I liked it that way. I missed seeing Victor in the hallway, but he did not exist anymore. I walked the hallways like a zombie and wished he had not saved me. I overheard some of my classmates talking about Brad, whom I had not seen since his confrontation with Victor. I asked Carly, and she told me that he had gone missing and no one knew where he was. I had an idea, what could have had happened to him, but I could not prove it, and people would think I had gone mad if I would tell them vampires were responsible for Brad's disappearance.

Being at school was a living nightmare for me, I did not want to be there, too many memories of Victor; everything reminded me of him. Some days, I would walk outside at the end of the day, expecting him to be there waiting for me. I missed him more than I thought I would, but I was still upset at him for being so selfish and not saving my mother, but I had to face the truth, he was gone for good, he was not coming back.

The days, weeks and months went by.

The school year ended. It was the beginning of summer. During all these months, I got close to some of the little orphans, a couple of them were placed with families, and new ones arrived at the orphanage. I was like a big sister to them, I would play with them, help them with their homework and as a treat, —I would read to them or tell them a story at night before sleeping.

Sister Delia somehow managed for me to attend the private school a block away from the orphanage, where some of the nuns thought classes.

It was my seventeenth birthday. I was feeling down and depressed, I missed my mother.

The orphans, each one had made a birthday card for me, and we celebrated my birthday with cupcakes, played musical chairs and danced to silly songs. Their company cheered me up.

"Amber," Sister Celeste called me. "This was dropped for you," she handed me a package wrapped in brown wrapping paper. Her dark olive skin made my hand look pale.

"Thank you."

The package did not say whom it was from, but I opened it. There were two books inside and a note that said, 'Happy Birthday, hope you enjoy the books'.

"Sister Celeste, ---did you see the person who dropped this?"

"No," her glasses slipped down her pointy nose, she pushed her glasses up with her index finger. "It was given to Sister Delia, she told me to give it to you."

"Oh, okay… thank you, Sister." I said with a gloomy sigh. After that, I ran upstairs to my room, I opened the closet and dragged the box I had brought with me and searched for the Romeo and Juliet book. I compared the handwriting on the note to the poem Victor wrote for me. It looked a lot like Victor's handwriting, if not the same, I said to myself and grinned, "he remembered my birthday," I muttered to myself.

While looking for the book I uncovered the letter my mother had written me right before she died. I sat down with the letter in my hand. I finally got the courage and opened it.

The letter read,
'My sweet Amber,

I had a long talk with Victor today; I know his secret, or what he is. He said that you had asked him to save me, but I do not want to be saved, he and Aubrey tried to convince me, call me old fashioned, but I want to die and stay dead. He also told me that you have agreed to marry him; I hope we have a chance to talk about this; I would love to hear it from you, to see the excitement on your face. I made him promise me that he will wait until you are at least eighteen to make you his bride. I am not opposed to you marrying him, I want you to be happy, and if that is what makes you happy I want you to go for it. Please don't be mad at him, he told me that you don't want to see him again; I know you and I really don't think you meant it, I had seen the love in your eyes when you look at him. I am writing you this letter because I do not know if I will see you again to talk to you about this in person, but in case I don't, I hope this letter makes you realize that Victor is a wonderful young man, he truly loves you Amber. Do not let love pass you by, true love only comes once, and I believe he is the one for you.

I am not too keen to find out he is a vampire, actually it's kind of hard to believe, but if he can keep you company and make you happy, I don't really care what he is as long as you love him and he loves you back.

I hope you understand that I am dying, this is God's decision and mine, and you should accept this. Don't blame Victor this is not his doing, he did try to talk me into becoming one of them, even if he was putting his life in danger just to prove his love for you.

Victor told me he is planning on leaving town soon, I hope you read this letter before he does and you are able to stop him. I want you to be happy. It is an order.

I can feel the end is near; I do not want you to miss me. Remember that I will always be with you

in your heart.
I love you so much,
Mom '

I wiped the tears from my eyes. I had finally learned the truth but it was too late, he was already gone. If I could see him again, I would apologize. I took out the music box he had given me, I opened the beautiful melody started to play. I closed it immediately. The memories were too painful, reminded me of my mother and Victor. I cried myself to sleep.

The days, weeks and months went by.

I liked the new school. On my spare time, I finished reading the books he gave me, and I re-read the ones I had on my eBook reader, the last present I got from my mother. It was a little bit outdated, but it still worked.

I found myself thinking of him more and more, daydreaming of what my future with him could have been. Almost every night, I would dream about him; those dreams felt so real, I did not want to wake up, especially when I dreamt of his butterfly kisses.

I woke up in the middle of the night from a vivid dream, so real I thought I saw Victor standing by the window, I turned on the little night lamp to take a good look but everything had been an illusion, the only weird thing was that I could smell his scent all over me. I turned off the lamp before the nuns would notice it. I walked to the window, it was cold outside, I could feel the cold air slipping inside the room through the old windows, the dark streets outside were dead and lonely like my soul.

I placed my hand on the window glass it was freezing cold, and with my breath I blew warm air on it, to make it fog and I drew a heart with my finger, inside I wrote the initials A -n- V.

I got back under the covers and went back to sleep, right back to my sweet dream with Victor.

It was the weekend, and as usual, I played with the kids. I took them outside to play in the snow. When the nuns called us back in, I noticed little Bobby was stunned looking at something in the distance.

I squatted down, "Hey what are you looking at?" I asked Bobby.

Only his freckled faced showed under the hood of his

oversized coat. "I saw Spiderman."

I snickered, "Where?"

"Over there," he pointed with his small hands.

I turned, "I don't see anyone Bobby."

"He... he jumped in and out really fast... and he.... and he climbed the wall," He was so excited he stuttered, his eyes wide opened, and he had a huge grin on his face.

I stood up and turned around again and I did not see anyone around the building. I glanced back at Bobby. "There is no one out there, I think Spiderman left," I grinned. "Come on lets go inside," I carried him up, "Whoa! ---you are getting too big for me."

"There he is Amber," he said excited and squirmed his little body around for me to put him down.

I turned around quickly. I was shocked. I placed Bobby down slowly. I was in a daze looking at Victor standing across the street. I felt my heart leap out of my chest. I wanted to run toward him. "Stay here Bobby," I then scurried to the fence.

Victor was wearing a black trench coat. He stood motionless, staring at me.

I was flabbergasted seeing him so close one more time. It was him, he had not changed one bit. This time it was real, it was not a dream, but I was speechless. I clutched onto the black iron bars.

"Amber."

I heard my name in the back and I turned around.

Sister Delia had called me. She was standing with Bobby.

I turned back and Victor was gone. I stood still for a moment, and then I headed back inside. I picked up Bobby, "don't tell anyone about Spiderman, okay?"

"You... you saw him too," Bobby stuttered.

"Yes, and it's our little secret... you see Spiderman is my friend."

Bobby grinned, "Okay, but next time, can I touch him?"

"Yes, you can." I smiled. I wanted to touch him too, but I could only hope that there was going to be a next time.

That night I looked out the window hoping to see him again. I fogged the window with my warm breath. I noticed there was another heart drawn next to the one that I had drawn the night before, but this one had written inside Victor loves Amber.

I smiled. He had been in my room, but I could understand

why he would not talk to me.   Why not take me with him.

    The days, weeks and months went by, it was summer again. I did not see nor had any other sign of Victor again. I had just finished my junior year. New kids were brought in, a few kids were adopted including little Bobby, which I really missed a lot. I had one more year of school to go before graduating, a few months away from my eighteenth birthday.

    At the end of summer, I started my senior year.

    Sister Delia gave me some money to buy clothes.   I went to the store without any chaperone. I had gained the nuns trust; they trusted me to return to the orphanage, my only home.

    I was shocked to see a flyer a couple of months old with Chloe's picture on the front, her parents were offering a reward for her safe return. First was Brad, and now Chloe, they both went missing.

    I went back to the orphanage and spent the rest of the day in my room wondering if Victor had anything to do with Chloe's disappearance.

    The months went by it was winter again and I turned eighteen. I did not get a present this year from Victor, and he did not come back for me as I figured he would. I was alone in this world and I did not like that feeling, so I kept myself busy with my studies and the orphans to keep those self-destructive thoughts from coming back and haunt me. It had been two years since I moved in to the orphanage. All of the orphans that were here when I arrived had already been placed in homes. I finally graduated from high school. Now it was my turn to move on and start a new life on my own.

CHAPTER 11

I finally moved out of the orphanage.

I used some of my mother's saving to get a room at an extended stay hotel. I went ahead and paid the next two weeks, just to allow me enough time to find work and an apartment. The hotel was not the best one in town, but it had the essentials.

That morning I went early to the store and bought a newspaper. I lay on my chest, my feet in the air, crossed behind my back, while I read the classified and circled in red the jobs that I was best qualified for, which were not that many. I was either going to end up as a waitress or a store clerk.

There was a knock on the door.

"Housekeeping," the woman yelled.

"Come back later please," I yelled back.

I held the marker between my teeth, while I turned the page.

There was another knock.

I rolled my eyes. Geez, didn't she hear me? I said to myself. "Come back later," I yelled again this time louder.

The following knock on the door was even louder.

"Oh come on," I got up to tell the housekeeping lady to come back later. I unlocked the door, "I am not…" I felt my jaw drop, when I saw Victor standing outside the door. My heart rose, beating faster than usual, I was elated to see him, I could hardly breathe, then after a moment of awkward silence I managed to say his name,

"Victor."

"May I come in Amber?" He smiled softly.

I could not blink, I was in a trance, I studied his face and was amazed that he had not changed at all, his skin, his lips and his mesmerizing eyes were just the same as I remembered. I wanted so badly to caress his face, "uhm... yeah... yes of course," I said in a jittery voice and let him in.

Victor stared at me, "you look beautiful."

"You haven't changed," I snickered.

He chuckled, "No."

"Uhm... how is Emma and Max?" I fidgeted with the marker in my hands. I walked to the bed to put away the newspaper, but his presence made me useless. I kept twisting the cap on the red marker.

He followed me with his eyes, "they are doing well."

"Your mom and dad?" I asked with my back facing him, I forced myself to relax, but my heart wanted to leap out of my chest. I turned around slowly and saw him grin.

"They are doing well too," he took a few steps closer and looked in my eyes, "you are nervous don't be," he lowered his gaze and slowly dislodged the marker away from my hands and threw it on the bed.

"How do you want me to act, I haven't seen you in a while?" I flipped my hair and slowly walked around him.

He put his hand on my shoulder, "I am not a stranger Amber."

The touch of his hand made my skin tingled, a warm feeling rushed through me, I felt the blood burning through my veins, it was like someone striking a match and relighting the fire that had been dormant for these few years. I could not let myself fall so easily, I was still mad at him for leaving me.

"Sort of, I haven't had contact with you these last two years, I saw you only one for a few seconds... and I..."

He wrapped his arms around me, and smiled, "Shh."

I shoved him, "You left me Victor."

"You told me to leave you alone."

"But you shouldn't have listened to me, --I was young and stupid," I said distressed.

"What?" He looked confused. He looked at me and shook his head. He then started to laugh.

"Don't laugh," I pouted. Seeing him laugh made me laugh too.

"Come here," he hugged me again, "I missed you, and your incoherent behavior."

"I missed you more," I gazed at him and got lost in his hazel eyes.

He shifted his gaze and meticulously studied my face, inch by inch. He softly said, "Amber I came for you."

"For me?"

"Yes. Do you still love me?" He asked warily.

I looked at him thrilled, "I do Victor, more than ever."

He slowly lowered his head and pressed his lips to mine, and kissed me in a way he had never done before, it was not even close to the kiss he gave in the lodge the night he told me his secret. The silky touch of his kisses turned hotter and more penetrating. My arms wrapped around his neck. He pressed me against his solid body, he slowly backed me up to the bed, I felt the edge of the bed against the back of my knees and I sat down.

He kneeled on the floor and continued to kiss me, there was a sweet invasion inside my mouth.

I tangled my fingers through his hair. "Victor," My heart was beating faster; I was breathless, struggling for air. I desired him. The passion I had kept all these years inside me was too strong. I lost control and desperately clung to him.

He took his shirt off, revealing his chiseled pale chest, "Amber, I promised your mom, I would wait, but not anymore. I can make you mine now. You are ready. I want to make love to you," he scooped me up laying my body completely on the bed.

A fervent desire rushed through my body. I wanted him. I started to unbuttoned my shirt.

"Let me do it." He gently undid the next button.

I watched him as he slowly undressed me. I just wanted him to rip them off, but he took his time and tenderly kissed every inch of my bare skin, until I was completely naked. He seemed ravished with delight when he saw my naked body, he then rapturously kissed my lips, we both were smoldering with desire. He pressed his hard body against mine. I was experiencing something I had never experienced before. I was alive in raw sensuality. Moments of pure bliss, his touch and kisses were setting off fireworks all around me. Our bodies heaved against each other. My body shifted restlessly beneath his attention. He moaned in gratification, I moved slowly and provocatively in response to his strokes. A feeling of euphoria overwhelmed me. I bit my lower lip to hold back a scream of pleasure. I was finally his. I softly smiled at him when he captured my gaze, my chest heaved uncontrollably.

He smiled back seductively, the corners of his mouth twisting upward. He looked elated, "You belong to me now."

"Is this when you kill me?" I asked innocently.

"No, not yet," he spoke softly.

"When?"

"Amber, I want to try something." He divulged.

"What?" I held the covers around my naked body.

"I want to start a family… I don't know if it will work."

"A family? Do you want to adopt a baby?"

"No, I want to see if you can have one."

"Is such a thing possible?"

"Yes," he said excited. "I have heard of it happening before, but usually is someone older, but you… you are young and fertile. I don't see that you would have any problems."

"But wait, you never said anything about that before." I said concerned.

"Since I left I have been planning this, and gathering information. Normally vampires date their own kind, but there have been times that they have had encounters with the living. And I found out that they have become pregnant and bore offspring…" He stopped.

"And? What happens to the babies?"

"They don't last too long… but it's because the mothers are usually older, not young and pure like you."

"Victor I don't know." The idea of being his guinea pig sounded crazy to me, I thought of the many things that could go wrong. I had a lot of thinking to do if I was going to consent to become part of his experiment.

"I'll make sure you have medical care through the pregnancy," he assured.

"And what happens to me?"

"Nothing… you wouldn't be in any danger."

"Are you sure?"

BUTTERFLY KISSES

"I am positive. I wouldn't dare put you in any harm."

"Hmm? —can I think about it?"

"Please Amber, that's all I ever wanted ---to have a family of my own, a wife and kids. That dream was taken from me the day I was viciously killed, but now there is a slight possibility that I can make it real."

There was a knock on the door.

"Housekeeping."

I chuckled, when I heard the lady at the door.

He smiled, "I guess is time to get dressed."

"Yes."

Victor took me out to eat. He asked for a glass of water, and watched me eat my hamburger. "I don't know how you can eat that," he wrinkled up his nose in disgust.

"These burgers are good, you should try one some time." I said with a mouth full.

"No thanks, I pass."

I saw the pained revolting look on his face. I snickered, "hey... I don't say anything about your diet."

"And you shouldn't because it will be yours pretty soon," he grinned.

"Yuk!"

We continued talking while I finished my greasy hamburger and fries. He told me that they were living in Alaska for now.

I thought that it was a little insane leaving the little sun we get here for everyday cold weather. I furrowed my eyebrows, "is that where we are going?"

"Yes."

"When do we leave?"

"The sooner the better, I can't stand much of the sun, the heat hurts my eyes, plus is kind of odd staying here during the summer when everyone is tanning and going to the river, and I look the way I do."

I was done with my burger, I could not take another bite. On our way to the car, I had a brilliant idea, "why don't we go to a tanning salon?" I suggested. I wanted him to spend some time with me before going to the cold frigid weather.

"I don't tan, Amber those tanning beds are not for us."

"Spray tan is," I grinned deviously.

"No, I am not doing that."
"For me," I smiled flashing my teeth.
"No."

Two hours later, we came out of the tanning salon. I had asked the girl for a natural tone, just a slight touch of color.

He did look different; his skin was not pale anymore.

I smiled, "See it wasn't so bad."

"I should have killed you when I had the chance," he said spiteful.

"Too bad," I said.

"Does it wash off?"

"Not immediately." I grinned.

"Do you know how much grief; Emma is going to give me? She did this once, and I was so mean to her I made fun of her for the longest time."

"Well you shouldn't have, if she gives you grief ---you had it coming."

Victor grunted.

"You look handsome, look at you. I really like it."

"I guess it's not so bad." He smiled seductively, "it looks natural," he slid his dark Ray Ban glasses on.

At the end of the day, we ended up at the hotel room. We spent the night together and the following couple of nights too. We continued to make love, expressing our love for each other. During the day we went swimming at the lake, we shared our time together doing things as normal people would do. I had a chance to apologize to Victor, I told him about my mother's letter. He confessed that he had been in my room at the orphanage as I had suspected. He also told me that he kissed me that night I woke up and saw him. I also learned from him, that he was the one that paid for the private school for me, and the extra money that Sister Delia would give me came from him. Finding out that he never completely left me, made me happy and bubbly inside. However, there was one thing that really shocked me, he told me that Sister Delia was a vampire like him and I never had a clue.

That night I snuggled next to him, I was finally happy and very much in love with a vampire. Then I realized that he was right, it was not just plain love I felt for him, —he was my soul mate —we belonged together. I spent the night planning a fake wedding in my head. I sighed. I wished we could get married for real and wear a white dress like the other girls. Instead, I was just going to have the traditional vampire wedding —a bite on the neck and I would belong to him. I continued fantasizing about having a real wedding, before falling asleep.

I woke up next morning, and Victor was gone. I sat up in bed, and looked around the room. Suddenly I had a knot in my stomach. I was scared of losing Victor, of being alone once again. I closed my eyes and wished for him to come back. I needed him because without him I was not complete.

Then the door opened and Victor walked in.

I jumped up and ran to him, I wanted to hug him, but he was carrying a white box. "Don't leave without telling me. You scared me."

"I am sorry... I am not going to leave you again." He placed a big white box on the slightly scratched and worn table by the window.

"Where did you go?"

"I had some people to see, and I got you something too."

"What is it?"

He picked up the white box and handed it to me, "I hope it fits."

I opened the big box, and pulled out a white sleeveless long dress, "What is this?"

"What does it look like? He asked with a smirk on his face.

"A wedding dress."

"Yes, your wedding dress."

I was surprised, "But... how did you know?"

"You talk on your sleep," he chuckled.

I pouted, "and you don't sleep," I said displeased. "I am sorry."

"Why are you sorry? You want to get married like a normal girl before starting a family and I respect that."

"I said that too?"

He smiled mischievously, "I asked you in your sleep."

I was embarrassed, and slumped back to bed covering my face with the covers.

"We are losing time, get up and get ready. We are meeting

Father Patrick, I convinced him to marry us in a rush."

"But we need a marriage license, don't we?"

"I got that too."

"How…"

He raised his eyebrow and gave me a cunning look.

"Never mind, I know," I said submissive. "Vampire mind control," I scoffed.

He smiled, "Hurry up we need to be there in an hour."

I did not know exactly where we were going, but he told me to take the dress with me. We arrived at a rose garden. I noticed the small white building in the middle, we walked toward it, and I saw that it was a chapel. Then I smiled with joy, when I saw that the Cromwells were there, it sure was a pleasant surprise to see my soon to be family there supporting us

Emma ran to me, you are not changed, where is your wedding dress?"

"It's bad luck," Victor said.

"I have it here in the box."

"She can change in the office," Victor said and then addressed Emma, "did you bring her the shoes?"

"Yes, got'em." Emma had a pair of white strappy shoes adorned with rhinestones in her hand.

I smiled. They seemed to have been running around getting everything ready at the last minute, and it was all for me to make my day special.

Emma and I ran to the annex building by the chapel and I quickly changed there with Emma's help.

"Ready," I said.

"Not yet we need flowers."

At that moment, Mrs. Cromwell entered carrying a small bouquet, and a matching vine crown completed with white and lilac flowers.

"Now you are ready, you look beautiful just like a fairy," Emma said and smiled pleased.

Mrs. Cromwell smiled and headed out the door, Emma followed.

"Emma, wait."

"Yes Amber."

"Don't make fun of his tan, please. I made him do it."

"I won't, I figured that was your idea," she grinned. "Hurry up your husband to be is waiting."

I was amazed the dress fit, it looked beautiful, a sleeveless long dress, it gathered at the front and flowed at the bottom. I raised my dress and looked at the shoes 'wow,' I said to myself, Emma really had good taste in fashion. I just hoped that I did not trip and break one of the straps, —they looked so delicate.

I met Victor at the altar. Father Patrick performed the ceremony, and pronounced us husband and wife.

The white gold ring he placed on my finger was unreal; I had never seen a diamond that big, it was a blinding emerald cut diamond with antique style patterns and engraving throughout the band.

Victor placed a soft gentle kiss on my lips, but I wrapped my arms around his neck and gave him a more passionate and unforgettable kiss.

I was his bride, tears of joy appeared in my eyes, but then those tears turned to sad tears, I missed my mother. I wanted to share this special day with her.

Victor understood my sadness and hugged me.

"She is in your heart, remember that," he said tenderly.

"I know she is." My voice cracked. I knew that my mom was watching me from heaven and wished she could be here with me.

"We are your family now, and we will have one of our own if everything goes to plan."

"Yes, I want that too." I was delightfully happy, but deep inside there was and will always be a tiny, but yet unfillable gap in my heart from missing my mom.

He lovingly looked into my eyes, "you have no idea how happy I'm feeling right now."

I could see the sparkle in his eyes, but his smile alone said it all. "Oh... I think I know, it shows," I leaned closer and kissed him again.

His family gathered around us, they hugged me and Victor. I was not alone anymore. I had a family.

That same day, his family returned to Alaska.

Victor and I spent our wedding night together in my hotel room, making love as husband and wife. This was my last night in Virginia. Victor promised we could return to Lexington, after I have been converted. He knew that one day I would like to visit my mother's resting spot.

I wore the locket Victor gave me on my sixteenth birthday. I opened and kissed the picture of my mother inside. "I will carry you with me always," I said aloud.

CHAPTER 12

I stared out of the plane's window, looking at the clouds pass by. Victor held my hand calming my nerves —this was my first time on a plane. I turned to glance at his gorgeous face. I had gotten so used to his cold, rigid hands, that it did not bother me anymore, I was happy and that's all that matter. I lost myself in his hazel eyes. I was finally living my dream, a beautiful sweet dream I never wanted to wake up. I rested my head on his shoulder, his sweet and alluring scent of his cologne was irresistible, I kissed his cheek and snuggle next to him and dozed off the rest of the flight until we landed at the airport in Anchorage, Alaska.

I was surprised the weather was not as cold as I had anticipated. I guess it was a good time to come during the summer when everything was green. It reminded me of home.

Victor had a car waiting for us at the airport. He opened the door for me, and waited for me to get in; he put the luggage in the trunk and got on the driver seat. We were ready to go to our new home.

"I'm not hearing you complaint, I guess you like it so far?" He said.

"Yes, I do, it sort of like being home."

"Well this is our new home now, so you better get used to the extremely cold weather and the dreaded long dark winters."

"But that won't bother me if I'm a vampire, right?" The thought of that day coming up soon made me smile. Soon I will be like him. We will be just like one.

He paused, "Of course not."

We headed away from downtown Anchorage and toward the mountains. After driving for more than half an hour through a scenic highway and watching the panorama of wild beauty, Victor pulled up on the driveway of a huge house sitting in the middle of nowhere, no other living persons within miles. Tall pine trees and other evergreens landscaping the lot surrounded the mansion. He stopped the car, "We are home," he smiled. He walked around to open the door for me.

I exited the car, "this is where we are going to live?"

"Yes, is there something wrong with it?"

"No, ---I am just surprised that's all. Does it come with a map?" I snickered and stared at the big mansion. Although, it was a pretty estate and extremely nice outside, it gave me the creeps, it reminded me of a haunted mansion.

"Silly, it only has seven bedrooms," he grinned. He reached for my hand, "come on they are expecting us."

Max opened the door; Emma, Estella and Aubrey were waiting by the end of the colossal stairwell.

"Victor, take your bride to your room, we will take care of the bags," Mr. Cromwell said.

"Come," Victor held my hand and I followed him up the stairs. Victor took me to the room, the first thing I saw as I walked in was a large Victorian style poster king size bed with luxury bedding decorated in a red and gold hues. Ruby red heavy silk drapes with gold fringes hanged on the windows, the drapes were drawn which let the sunlight in the room. I saw the bookcase on the wall with several books, and a cold fireplace that had not seen fire in a long time. The rest of the furniture was antique, the tables, the chairs, everything was. I felt like I had travel back in time to the Renaissance era.

"You don't like it?" Victor asked after seeing the objectionable expression in my face.

"No, it's beautiful… just not my taste but if you like it," I said awkwardly.

"The furniture has been in my family for a while, ---actually a very long time," he smiled. "I can have the room refurnished, if you like?"

"No," I wrapped my arms around his neck. "I am happy with it, honest. ---I just need to get used to certain things, but as long as I'm with you I know, I'll adjust easily." I ran my fingers through his hair; I gazed deeply into his eyes and told him how much I loved him.

He declared his love for me again.

My ears would never get tired of hearing him say how much he loved me and how much I meant to him. He sealed his pledge of eternal love to me with sweet tender kisses on my lips.

I promised myself to do my best to get used to being a vampire's wife and their unusual way of living.

Weeks went by.

Victor was not letting me out of his sight. I became his prisoner in that huge mansion. I did not interact with the outside world. At first, I did not mind as long as I was with him, but then everything changed, Victor started to leave me alone in our bedroom for longer periods of time. The solitude was getting to me, I felt like Victor was alienating me, I saw him less and less, while I stayed locked in the room without being able to escape.

Emma unlocked the door.

I was standing by the window trying to get a few sunrays and listening to the peaceful trickling water from the creek outside.

"Hi Emma," A soft smile appeared on my face, it was nice to see someone.

"Hey, how are you?"

"I don't know, you tell me, ---have I done something wrong?"

"No," she grabbed me by the arm, I had gotten used to their cold touch. We walked to the bed and she sat next to me.

"Then tell me why Victor hasn't come."

"He is not here, Amber. He is trying to arrange a doctor to move in with us."

"Why?"

"You know... he is trying to start a family with you," she explained.

"But how come he has me locked in here, ---like his prisoner and not his wife." My voice cracked, I wanted to cry. They were tears of anger and frustration of not knowing what he was up to.

"He just wants to keep you safe, while he is away."

"But he didn't tell me he was going away," My eyes welled.

"Don't cry… it's just that it has taken him longer than he thought."

"But what is the big deal with having a family, am I not enough for him?"

"A family has always been a big deal for him, that's why he made us."

My eyes widened surprised, "he made you?" I sniffled.

"Yes, Victor is my maker… he wanted a sister."

I frowned, "but he told me…" I paused and tried to remember every detail he confessed to me about his past. "Who made Estella and Aubrey?" I asked.

"Well he did, who else? He is our maker."

I gulped, "Uhm, but you did convert Max, right?"

"No, I couldn't --I asked Victor to do it for me he has more experience than me. We are vicious by nature but when it comes to someone you love, it's hard to do it ---you get scare that you might over do it and screw up," she explained.

"I see," I was uncovering the truth about Victor, the man I loved. I was not sure if I should be scared of him now, I still loved him, but I had a smidgen of doubt about his true feelings, just enough to worry me.

"I thought you had this conversation with Victor already," she looked puzzled.

"I did… but it was his version… not what you are telling me." I grinned.

"Oh!" She covered her mouth with her hand. "I am sorry. I shouldn't have opened my mouth," she said apologetic.

"Don't be Emma… it is best that I know the truth about my husband, no matter how horrible it is."

"I better go, if he knows I came to see you, I am going to get in a lot of trouble with him," she stood up and walked toward the door.

"Emma, wait! Can I go outside, just for a bit, —please. I'm tired of being locked between these four walls. I'm going crazy… I need some fresh air, ---look at me I'm as pale as you are," I showed her my pasty white arms.

She chuckled.

"Please," I begged.

"Ok, let's go ---no one is home right now. Just don't tell him I let you out."

"Promise," I smiled and I sneaked outside with her.

We went for a short walk outside. I took deep breaths and closed my eyes. I enjoyed the cool breeze, and the few sunrays peeking through the giant pine trees. I was enjoying a few minutes of freedom. Then I heard what it sounded like a cracking tree branch, it startled me and I turned around, there was a black bear and her cub walking in the woods.

"Amber, turn around and walk slowly back to the house, I'll take care of it," Emma cautioned.

I did as she told me, I slowly back away and went inside. I sat at the base of the colossal stairwell and waited for Emma. I looked around the enormous house; it was cold and empty, as empty as the void I had in my heart since Victor left.

The door flew open, it sounded like if someone had kicked it in. I was ready to flee when I saw Emma walk in, blood dripped from the side of her mouth. Her jeans stained with blood and mud.

I looked in shock at the gruesome sight.

She wiped the blood from her mouth, "Sorry."

"What happened?"

"The bear won't be bothering us anymore."

"You took on the mama bear?" I said amazed by her skills, she had just killed a bear and did not have a scratch.

"Yes and the cub too… their blood is actually good, better than elk."

I gasped, "but the cub was adorable, it wasn't going to hurt us."

"The cub was an appetizer. I'm going to go change and you need to get back to your room before Aubrey and Estella get back."

Her nonchalant and lack of emotions did not surprise me much, but I still felt a bit disgusted knowing that this was the life I had chosen and it was too late to back down. I tried to understand their savage instinct, but since I still had a soul, it was hard for me to comprehend the life of a vampire. The only thing I could do was to wait until I became one, and maybe then, I will get it.

That night Victor returned home to me. He unlocked the door

and walked in the room, I lay in bed with a book. I sat up when I saw him. My love had just walked in. He was dressed all in black again, something I had noticed since we moved in the mansion, he had been wearing dark clothes, he looks very handsome and provocative but it gives him a mysterious edge especially because I know he is a vampire. I wondered if he was expecting me to dress like a black widow, once I become a vampire. My lips curled in an amused grin at the ironic thought.

He ran to my side and kissed me on the lips; however, I did not kiss him back. I was upset at him for lying to me and for keeping me prisoner, the way he had.

"What took you so long?" I pounded him on the chest, "and why didn't you tell me, you are their maker?" I reproached.

He grabbed my wrists holding my hands still, "who told you?"

"It doesn't matter who told me, you lied."

He let go of my hands, "If I had told you, would you have taken me as your husband? I don't think so, you were terrified of me."

"No I wasn't," I said swiftly.

"Really? ---You should have seen your face, and that is not saying anything about how fast your heart was beating."

"But you should have let me make that decision on my own ---with the truth, not a lie."

"So now you know, I am a vicious sadistic killer… do you still want to be with me?"

"I don't know… I don't like you lying."

"I'm sorry… you don't know what I have gone through, I had just found you, my true love and I wasn't going to scare you away," he seemed sincere.

"No more lies?"

"No more lies, I swear. Now you know everything there is to know about me," he said.

With his charming pleasing ways, he won me again. His kisses reminded me why I had married him. I was unconditionally in love with him. I was his soul mate and will be for an eternity.

He caressed the inside of my leg, although his hands were cold, a warmth feeling rushed through my body upon his contact, he pressed his hard toned body against mine, and he traced my neck and shoulders with butterfly kisses.

He placed a soft gentle kiss on my lips, his kisses were hungrier and more passionately. He dropped kisses all over my face and neck. He then did what I was longing for, he bit me. I could feel his sharp teeth penetrating my skin. He sucked in my blood, a feeling of euphoria inundated my body and mind. A rush of passion ran through my veins, my heart pounded, I let out a whimpering cry for him to stop, but I was shamefully enjoying his bite. He licked the bite wound. I was shaking all over. I wanted him. The desire overcame the pain.

"Is this it?" I gasped for air and stared at him.

"No," he spoke softly. "Not yet... I just couldn't control myself any longer and I had to taste you... next time it won't be like this," he admitted.

"Why don't you get it over with and change me?"

"Not yet," he repeated and placed a kiss on my lips silencing me.

I eased my hands down his chest, and adored him with my touch. My lips parted and I kissed him, an enticing invitation that he took, he latched his mouth on mine.

"I want you," he muttered hoarsely as his hands skillfully stroked my naked body underneath the white sheets.

Every movement was pulling me, dragging me closer to him, teasing me with hints of mindless ecstasy, until I could not resist anymore. I shuddered in between the sheets, and clutched unto his shoulders. A tidal wave of immense pleasure pushed me over the top, to the point of no return. Ripples of ecstasy flooded his body and he jerked. He buried his face in my shoulder to muffle his shout. Then he pressed his cheek against mine, and whispered in my ear, "I love you."

"Not more than I do." I whispered back.

"That's impossible," he brushed away the hair from my face and gave me a sweet and tender smile followed by a kiss.

That night he spent it with me in the room. I did not want to fall asleep I was afraid he would leave again, but my eyelids betrayed me as they got heavier and finally drooped with weariness.

The morning light hit my face, and I opened my eyes. I turned around and reached for Victor, but only touched the empty bed. I was alone. Victor had left me again. I hugged the pillow, and started to cry. Then I heard someone at the door, and I raised my head from the pillow. Suddenly I felt like my heart started beating again and I wiped the tears from my eyes.

Victor came in to the room carrying a breakfast tray, "good morning."

I ran to the door, "you didn't leave…" I smiled.

"No, I went to get you something to eat," he stared at me, "were you crying?" He walked to the table to put the tray down.

"No." I grinned.

"Liar, your nose gives you away every time."

"I'm ok now, —it smells delicious," I changed the subject I did not want to get into my insecurities.

He narrowed his eyes, and smiled, "I got a new cook for you. Well she will be more than that, —she'll be tending to your needs. Her name is Olga. She is the daughter of Dr. Abendroth your new doctor. Olga will keep you company when I am not here."

"Why wouldn't you be here? ---Victor I am getting tired of you leaving me alone, it is as if you married me to keep me captive just for your crazy experiment… I didn't sign up for that."

"Wanting to have a family, it's not a crazy experiment," he looked offended.

"Under your circumstances, it is or did you forget you are dead?"

Victor turned around and walked away non-responsive.

I ran and hugged him. "I'm sorry, I didn't mean it, —it's just that I have dependency issues and I need you with me to feel complete."

He turned around to face me, "I'm sorry too baby. The reason I keep you inside these four walls is because, I don't want anything happening to you. You are a fragile little human, in a house occupied by vampires… surrounded by predators out in the forest, you are no longer in the suburbs of Virginia. If I am not here I can't protect you," he gently touched my face.

"But your family likes me, they won't hurt me," I stared at his penetrating eyes.

"Amber my love, don't be so naive, we are cold hearted blood sucking creatures of the night, none of that matters. To them I'm their maker and they will listen to me, but I can't be too sure that they won't turn against you in my absence, if for instance you would get a cut or you are having your period," he paused and hugged me pressing me against his body. "They are my family but I love you more and if one of them would hurt you, I would not even blink before I rip their heads off."

"I love you too, and I do understand what you are saying," my fingers played with his hair, "but you have to understand me," my eyes would not leave his. "You want to have an offspring, and believe me I would love to give you the family you always wanted… but I am not getting pregnant, Victor, and to tell you the truth I don't think is going to happen." My words hurt him, I saw it in his eyes, and it was heartbreaking. I had failed him. I could not give him what he wanted, but I really do not think it was my fault.

His gaze dimmed. He sighed and followed with a mirthless smile, "I'll make you a deal, if by the end of winter you are not pregnant, I will change you."

"That's a long wait."

"Please just give me until then."

I nodded agreeing to the impossible.

A month went by Victor did not go anywhere. He stayed home with me. He finally introduced me to Olga; she was a tall, rail thin girl with reddish hair. To my surprise, she was human like me, and way stronger than she appeared. She started to bring me my daily meals. She was very quiet, and when she spoke she spoke softly and servile with a foreign accent.

I continued to be a captive in my room, with no contact with the outside world. I was the perfect victim, a lonely girl with no family or friends, no one to miss me.

Victor would come and stay in the room with me almost every night, except for those he had to go hunting. In the time living with Victor, I have learned something disturbing, unlike the rest of his family, Victor craved more human blood than animal. He would travel to nearby towns to find a victim at least once a month to satisfy his thirst.

The nights we spent together, he would hug me until I fell asleep. I think he knew I wanted to feel him close, that every night I fought to stay awake, so he would not leave. I think he finally understood what it meant to be husband and wife, and he started to sleep in our room every night.

I finally got what I wanted. We continued our normal life as a married couple, if you could call being alone most of the day and married to a vampire normal. During our lovemaking, Victor could not resist the temptation of biting me. On a couple of occasions he over did it, and I would faint, he would then need to feed me a few drops of his blood to snap me out of it. At the beginning, I was disgusted, but now, I had developed a taste for his blood.

Weeks went by, and then one morning, Victor woke me up, he had his ear pressed against my stomach.

"What are you doing?" I asked confused.

"Shh!"

I stayed quiet, trying to figure out what he was doing.

He lifted his head and met my gaze. He smiled softly and had a thrilled look on his face.

"What?"

"I'm glad I brought the doctor with me… I think you are expecting."

My eyes widened, "I'm what?"

"You are carrying my offspring, Amber… I can hear a heartbeat apart from yours, it's faint and echoing ---but I can hear it," his eyes sparkled with joy.

CHAPTER 13

The months past, it was early to mid Spring. The drab landscape outside my window was replaced by fresh green of spring seemingly overnight. Cotton grass and white blossoms of dwarf dogwood had begun to cover the forest floor. I could spot tiny blue bouquets of forget-me-not near the trail by the creek.

I gently touched my overly extended belly. I could feel the babies kick. I was carrying twins. I was shocked when the doctor told me; I did not even know twins ran in our families. I was under the care of Dr. Abendroth. On Victor's request, the doctor would check on me every two weeks. Dr. Abendroth was human too, a chubby pear shaped man, with a bald spot on top of his head and very little hair left. He wore dark rimmed glasses that were held up in place by his huge nose. The doctor did not seem to be bothered by Victor's presence or the fact that his daughter, Olga lived in a house filled with vampires.

Victor stopped feeding on me. His fang marks on my inner thighs, arms and neck had healed but the scars were a constant reminder of his thirst for me. He was not the only one that craved blood, I also did, through the months I had developed a taste for his droplets of blood.

I was treated like a porcelain doll. I was forbidden to leave the room by myself, the only way I could step a foot outside the bedroom door was with him and no one else.

I heard someone struggling to get the door open.

"Oh it's you," I said disappointed when I saw Olga.

She walked in carrying a tray in her hand, "yes ma'am, I am bringing you your supper ---I hope you like what I made for you," she bowed her head and stared at the floor as she walked by me. She placed the tray on the small table facing the window.

"Is there anything else ma'am?" She glanced down. She would not make eye contact with me.

I cocked my head to the side and scoffed, "have you seen my husband?"

"No ma'am, no one is home right now, they all left," she spoke softly with her foreign accent.

"I see," I paced around in my maternity white gown and walked to the table to check out what she had brought me to eat, "Do you mind leaving the door open, I am going for a little walk when I'm done."

Olga stopped at the door, "I am not allowed ma'am. I have orders to keep the door locked at all times."

I lifted my chin in the air, "but you serve me, and I'm telling you to leave the door open," I picked up the steak knife from the table and concealed it behind my back. I started to feel weird, a sudden flare of rage, I fell under a haze. Seconds later, I snapped out from the darkness, and realized that I had charged at Olga with the knife. I had her pinned down against the wall, with the sharp blade against her throat.

Her terrified eyes finally facing me, "but ma'am, ---I can get in a lot of trouble with your husband," her voice quivered.

After seeing the terrified look on her face, I felt remorse and guilt. I stepped back and let her go, "I am sorry Olga. I don't know what got into me."

She scurried out the door before I could say anything else and quickly locked the door from the outside.

I dropped the knife on the floor and walked away from the door. I sat on the edge of the bed, trying to figure out why I had snapped like that.

Then I heard the door unlock, but no one came in.

I stood up and slowly approached the door. I tested the doorknob and it was unlocked, and I let myself out. I saw Olga standing at the end of the hall, she lowered her head and turned around and walked to her room. I sneaked downstairs but I did not see anyone. I freely walked outside to the creek. It was relaxing to listen to the water rolling down the creek. I sat on the stone bench under the trees. I took deep breaths of fresh air and admired the scenery, the chirping of the birds, the fragrance of the blooming flowers I was taking it all in, making a memory before the sun would set and I had to go back to my cell.

I felt free and happy. I could feel the twins moving inside my huge belly, they were moving more than usual today. I pressed my hand on my belly to calm them down.

I thought of different names for them. I held the locket with my mother's picture, reflecting on how happy my mom would be if she had the chance to meet them. I decided to name the girl Savannah, after my mother. I lost track of time, I had stayed out longer than I was expecting. The sun had started to fade, but the dusky sky was still fairly well lit. I headed back to the house, I stopped when I saw Victor's car parked outside. "Oops, I am in trouble," I said to myself and hurried up back in.

When I sneaked in, I could hear Victor yelling at Olga. I hurried my steps up the colossal stairs as fast as I could manage with the huge belly I carried, wobbling back and forth like a penguin.

"Stop!" I yelled. "Leave her alone."

Victor turned around, "Where were you? How did you get out?"

"I'm okay," I pushed him and walked in to our room.

"Get your things and leave this house immediately," he ordered Olga. He followed me in to the room and slammed the door.

"It wasn't her fault," I raged.

"I left you under her care, and I come back and you are not in the room."

"I went for a walk, ok?"

"But you know you are not allowed."

"You are keeping me prisoner again, and I don't like that."

"Amber, you can hurt the babies if you fall or something."

"Oh the babies… so you are not concerned about my welfare, huh?"

"I didn't say that."

I scoffed, "sure that's all you wanted me for, —I'm your

personal incubator."

He raised his eyebrows, "Don't say that. You know that's not true."

"It is the truth Victor, just admit it!"

"You are mad at me."

"You think? What gave me up?" I was furious, I was yelling. The sound of my footsteps echoing as I paced to and fro, then I felt a stabbing pain in my stomach, "Ouch!" I doubled over in pain.

"What is it?" Like a lightning bolt, he rushed to my side.

I grunted, "I... I don't know?" I said taking fast shallow breaths. "Get the doctor?" I looked at him.

He had a frantic look on his face. He then yelled for Olga.

Olga came in. "Yes, Sir."

"Stay with my wife, I have to go get your dad."

She nodded, and helped me to the bed.

"I'm sorry Olga for getting you in trouble," I said gasping for air.

"It's okay ma'am, you need to rest."

Then Victor rushed in with Dr. Abendroth.

The doctor checked me and asked Victor to step outside the room.

I looked at the doctor, "why does he have to go?" I asked taking in uneven breaths. "Aaah!" I screamed again with discomfort, I felt another stabbing pain. I pressed my hand on my stomach.

"Because you are having the babies, and I don't know how he will react with the blood."

"You mean I'm having the twins now?" My eyes bulged out. It could not be. I was not due yet.

"Yes, you are in labor, --don't worry Olga is going to help."

The pain was excruciating, the contractions were getting closer and more frequently. I felt as if my hips were being pulled apart.

Olga kept wiping the sweat from my forehead with a small towel. After two hours of labor, I was exhausted and ready to pass out, and shortly after that, the twins were born.

Olga cleaned them and wrapped them in their pink and blue blankets to identify each one.

The first one she handed me was little Savannah, she was tiny and her face was red, her small fingers and hands looked wrinkled like an old person. Then Olga handed me the boy, I had no name for him yet, I decided to call him Victor after his dad.

The twins were tiny but seemed healthy, just like any regular baby.

Olga helped me change to my robe, taking my bloodstain gown away. She also changed the sheets, before I lay down again. I saw them put the bloody sheets and garments in black plastic bags. "What are you going to with that?" I asked.

"We have to burn them," Dr. Abendroth looked at me.

"Doctor, why do you work for them? Aren't you scared of them?"

"No. I have known Victor for a long time. He has taken care of me since I was a little boy. He has been sort of like a dad to me," he said with his foreign accent.

"Oh... I see."

"I am very happy for him. He finally gets to have his own children... I have to get him now, so he can meet them, would you excuse me?" he smiled.

I nodded, "doctor before you go..." I took a deep breath of bravery, "do you think my twins are normal?"

"By normal, do you mean human?"

I nodded, "uh huh."

"Yes, they have a heartbeat, and their body temperature is normal like any other infant. But we need to keep a closer look, just in case anything goes wrong," he then turned to Olga. "Olga, take the trash bags out please to the backyard and burn them."

"Yes, papa," she carried out the bags with her scrawny arms.

I held the twins, one in each arm.

Victor cautiously opened the door, and seemed to be petrified to see us.

"Come on in, they don't bite," I chuckled after seeing his face expression.

He slowly walked toward us, and sat next to us on the bed, his eyes glancing back from one baby to the other. A single drop of blood rolled down his cheek.

"Are you crying?" I asked.

He nodded without an articulate response.

"Cat got your tongue?" I smiled.

He giggled nervously, "they are mine?" He looked at me with loving eyes.

"Meet Savannah Maria and this little fellow over here is Victor Antonio."

"You named him after me?"

"Of course, you're his dad."

I handed him Savannah, who was snuggly wrapped in her pink blanket.

"She is warm," he smiled. "And her heart is beating," he said surprised. He kissed Savannah's forehead, and then looked at me. "You gave her my mother's name too."

"Yes."

"She is beautiful, Amber. Just like you."

"They both are gorgeous. Thank you," I admired their tiny faces.

"Why are you thanking me?" He asked.

"For giving me this gift, you have made me so happy," I touched his cold face with my free hand. I finally had something that was mine. They were a part of me and they would never leave me.

"I am glad you agreed to do this, now I have what I always wanted, because of you. I love you Amber," he leaned closer and gave me sweet butterfly kisses on my lips as he did so many times.

"I love you too."

We were interrupted by a knock on the door, and then Estella poked her head in, "may we come in?"

"Of course," I answered.

Estella, Mr. Cromwell, Emma and Max walked in to welcome the babies.

Estella was the first one to approach us.

Victor stood up proudly and handed her little Savannah.

"Oh my--- they are warm," she said surprised.

"Yes," Victor grinned.

"They are not…" She stopped and looked at me.

"I don't think they are, but the doctor said that we should watch them carefully in case there is any change," he answered her question.

"Aww, look at their red faces, they look scrumptious," Emma said.

"Emma!" I reproached.

Victor narrowed his eyes and growled at Emma.

"I didn't mean it that way, ---I meant to say that they are adorable, just gorgeous... I am glad they take after their mother," she rolled her eyes at Victor.

Victor scoffed and did not find her statement amusing.

She chuckled, "Oh come on little brother," Emma said to Victor. "May I carry one, please?"

Victor thought about it for a moment, "just make sure you keep your fangs away from them, or else."

"You know I wouldn't dare."

Victor handed little Victor Antonio to Emma.

"I say it again --I am glad they look like Amber," Emma teased Victor.

"I named him after Victor," I told Emma.

"And why would you do such a thing, you couldn't think of a better name?"

"Keep it up Emma," Victor said harshly.

"Well you offended me first... you shouldn't have thought that I would hurt my niece and nephew."

Max touched their little hands, "they sure are cute!"

"I am very happy for you Victor," Mr. Cromwell threw his arm around Victor and gave him a tight squeeze.

Victor laughed. His face filled with happiness, no one could erase that proud smile from his face.

"Yes, you finally got what you wanted, your own family," Estella smiled.

The twins started to cry.

Emma looked startled by their cry, and quickly handed me little Victor, "here I don't know what to do."

Estella rocked little Savannah. "I think they may be hungry."

"What do we feed them?" Victor asked Estella.

Estella glanced at me.

"Hmm, I guess I should feed them? ---but I don't know how exactly," I said.

"Why don't you give it a try, we will step outside," Estella suggested.

Victor walked with them to the door.

"Victor, don't go," I stopped him.

"I'm not; I'm just locking the door."

"You still don't trust them?"

"Can never trust a vampire."

I laughed, "Tell me about it."

He grinned.

I managed to breast feed the twins and we put them in the bassinets that Victor had brought from the nursery room.

Victor kept guard of us day and night. He would not leave us not even to go feed.

A couple of weeks had gone by. The twins did not show sign of being anything but human their temperature had not dropped nor their nourishment habits had changed.

Victor was pacing around carrying little Victor in his arms, while I changed Savannah's diaper.

We went for our daily walk outside. Victor pushed the double stroller.

I stopped, "Victor, I have been meaning to ask you... when are you going to turn me?"

"Can we talk about that later?"

"Why not now?" I asked.

"What's the rush?" He spoke tightly. My question seemed to have bothered him.

"I am not in a rush, but you said you would, --- besides I want to live forever with you."

"Amber," he gently touched my face, and looked into my eyes with those piercing hazel eyes. "I can't do it anymore," he shook his head.

"Why?"

"The twins, ---when I thought of having them, I figured they would turn out to be a little more like me, --but when I heard their little hearts beating and blood flowing through their tiny veins —everything changed, Amber, I can't take their mother away."

"But you are not, ---you are giving me eternal life, I would still be able to take care of them."

"And what about them, huh? I will not be able to turn them. I would rather have my head and limps ripped off, than to kill my own children, besides they are so tiny something can go wrong," he said anguished. "Please let's not talk about it again," he walked away.

I saw the torment in his eyes, I had no idea he felt that way. I caught up with him and gave him my word, I would never ask him to turn me nor the twins again.

A few months went by. The twins were three months old now. They were getting chubby, but they still seemed very fragile to me. Victor finally had come around and was letting me go out with the twins, as long as I was in the company of one the Cromwells. He seemed to trust them a little more around me and the twins.

Most of the times I went with Emma, we liked going shopping to the nearest city, she enjoyed getting stuff for the babies. Today, we decided to go to a different city a little further away, so this time we took longer than we had anticipated. The sun had already set; we were in an unfamiliar, dark and narrow road. The flapping sound of the windshield wipers and the rain on the rooftop of the car contributed to the background noise of the tires rolling on the wet pavement. I was a little concerned about the sleek look of the asphalt road, I looked back at the twins, but the little angels were sound asleep in their car seat.

Emma slowed down, when she sensed my fear. We continued with our conversation, suddenly the headlights from the vehicle behind us blinded us; Emma looked through the rearview mirror. "What's his deal?"

"May be you should let him pass." I said to Emma.

The other vehicle sped up and passed us, then suddenly swerved in front of us and slammed on the brakes as if something had just run in front of it.

Emma tried to swerve but lost control of the car. The car rolled over several times and I passed out.

I woke up later in my room when I heard voices around me, I had no idea how long I had been out. My head hurt, my whole body ached, and I felt weak.

I heard Dr. Abendroth voice, he was talking to Victor. Victor's back was toward the bed, but I knew it was him; he was wearing his black sweater and dark jeans. I saw Emma and Estella in the room. Each one was carrying one of the twins.

"Victor, she is opening her eyes."

I heard Mr. Cromwell said.

Victor rushed to my side. He held and kissed my hands,

"How are you feeling?"

"Everything hurts," my voice sounded frailty. "Are the twins ok?"

"Yes, they are," Victor, answered distressed.

I coughed and I covered my mouth with my hands. I felt my hands wet, I looked at my hands they were covered with blood.

"Everyone leave the room, please," Victor ordered.

"What's wrong with me, Victor?" I uttered softly.

Victor did not answer me.

I turned my head toward the door, and saw everyone leave the room.

"Why are they taking the twins? ---Victor, answer me!"

"Shh…" He leaned closer, "let me kiss your warm lips one last time, you are not going to hurt anymore," he dropped kisses on my lips.

"Save me Victor," I looked into his eyes for what it seemed to be the last time.

"I love you —I always will," he sunk his fangs on my neck, this time felt different from the other times. I gasped for air, I wanted to cry, and scream in agony but he was sinking his fangs deeper and deeper. "It hurts Victor, please stop!" I uttered. The pain I was feeling was agonizing, my guts felt like they were on fire. I started to lose consciousness, my body was frigid cold, I could hear the rhythm of my heartbeat slowly fading, and then I blacked out.

CHAPTER 14

From above I saw Victor hugging my lifeless body. I could not hear what he was saying. I could only feel the anguish he was experiencing. It was like watching a silent movie.

I looked around me, everything was dark, then I heard a whimsical voice say my name, I have heard that voice before.

"Amber, ---Amber ---this way."

I followed the voice in the dark. The same voice I heard since I can remember, I could not never forget that voice. I yelled, "mom... is that you?"

"Amber this way."

Her voice guided me. I finally reached the end of the dark tunnel, and entered a bright cool place, where everything was white and serene.

A woman's figure protruded out of the snow-white surroundings.

"Mom?"

"Amber," she smiled, "my sweet baby."

She had a milk white gown, which seemed to swirl and dance in the wind. Her long brown hair flowed over her shoulder, making her face glow. She was healthy with rosy cheeks, and dewy lips. Her skin glittered. She looked beautiful, just like an angel would.

"Mom," I ran to her and hugged her, "but how is this

possible?"

"Just believe it is… we don't have much time to get into details," she kissed my forehead.

"Why?"

"You must go back."

"But why… I want to stay," I felt peaceful being in her presence.

"You have a family now to take care of… turn around," she pointed behind me, "I believe he needs you," she said caring.

I turned at her command. I saw Victor like a projection on the white background. He was still hugging my lifeless body, rocking it back and forth. I then saw him rest my body back down on the bed. He kissed me and walked away. He seemed lonely and miserable, carrying inside and empty lost soul.

"He is truly in love with you, and he is missing you, Amber. He thinks he has killed you."

"But he did," I replied.

"No, you were dying already from the accident. That is why I am here. I was coming to get you."

"But I didn't die from the accident, he bit me."

"I know, this is Victor's doing ---but somehow he keep you alive for those hours until he found the strength to turn you. If he had not bitten you then, you would not have gotten a second chance."

"If my time is not up yet, why am I here then?"

"It was your lack of will to live. Don't think I don't know you tried to kill yourself."

I lowered my head ashamed. "But…"

She sighed. "I see you haven't changed much, there are no buts ---I am telling you, you have to go back."

"Mom but I want to stay with you," I hugged her.

She chuckled. "I would love for that to happen too… but you don't belong in this world, Victor needs you and the twins need you."

I took a step back, "You've seen them?"

"Yes I have, they are precious."

"The girl is named after you," the thought of them lighted up my spirit with joy. I had more than one reason to go back. They needed me, the same way I needed my mother. I had to return to them.

"Yes, I know, little Savannah," she smiled, "I have always

been around," she placed her hand against my chest. "I am in your heart, Amber, where I'll always be ---no matter what you are now."

My eyes welled knowing that I had to leave her again, but I knew I had to go.

"That's your family now," she said.

I looked again at the silent projection of Victor holding the twins.

"Will I ever see you again?"

"No, honey… this is goodbye."

Tears flowed down my cheeks.

She hugged me tight, "Go on… follow your heart, you will find your way back."

A strong force was pulling me. The love I had for the twins was more powerful than anything else in the atmosphere. My motherly love was stronger than the love I felt for Victor. I entered the black tunnel and proceeded leaving my mom behind in the light.

I continued to see Victor in the distance, and then I moved closer and closer. My dead soul reentered my lifeless body, and I opened my eyes. I heard Emma's voice —she was talking to Victor. I turned my head to the side to look toward where the voices were coming from.

"Victor," I uttered his name.

Victor ran to me and hugged me, "What took you so long?" He kissed me all over my face, stopping at my lips for a deep kiss. "I love you so much, don't you ever leave me again," he whimpered.

"Welcome back Amber," Emma said. "I'll leave you two lovebirds alone."

"Where are the twins?" I asked.

"Estella took them to their room," Victor answered.

"I thought this is their room too."

"Not anymore, the twins are not human as we all thought. They survived the accident without a scratch."

"Is that why you bit me?"

"No, I didn't want to lose you, you were dying my love, I kept giving you droplets of my blood to keep you alive, but that wasn't enough, you were bleeding internally, —I was losing you," Victor explained.

I noticed him holding something in his hand; it looked like a tiny glass bottle, "What's that?"

"This? ...this is my ticket out," he snickered, "I guess I won't need it anymore," he stood up and walked to the bookcase, there he reached for a book and hid the vial inside of the book.

"What is it?" I asked puzzled.

He turned around, "Its poisoned blood."

"Poisoned?"

"Well for vampires it is, ---it is the cursed blood of one of the original vampire priest, mixed with holy water."

"Do I get one too?" I asked.

He explained to me that only he and Emma had one, and how hard it was for them to obtain it and that it had been in their possession for a long time.

"Why did you have it in your hands?" I asked warily.

"I thought I had lost you... I felt empty inside," he sat back down on the bed next to me.

"What about the twins? Were you going to leave them alone?"

"How could I explain to them that I killed their mother, I couldn't live with that guilt." A blood teardrop rolled down his face.

"Are you crying?"

He scoffed, "Sorry," he wiped it off.

I chuckled. "Vampires crying is not cute at all."

"Vampires huh? ---You are one of us now," he gave me a wicked smile. "That reminds me, you need to feed, ---here drink some of my blood we need to finish the transformation," he pierced his arm with his fangs.

The sight of blood attracted me. I immediately latched my teeth into his arm, and started to suck the blood from him, more than I ever had before.

Victor groaned, "Ok I think you got enough."

I licked my lips, "but I'm still hungry."

"I know, come on lets go hunt something for dinner."

"I want to see the twins, first."

"You will," he kissed me softy and then became more aggressive, and we forgot about dinner.

Each of his kisses and strokes lead me closer to the boiling point of ecstasy. There was not an inch of me that he did not taste, —from the base of my throat to the curve of my waist. He pressed his hard toned body against mine. He pleasured me. I tangled my fingers in his hair and I arched my hips as the tremors of pure ecstasy ruled and shook my body. My body convulsed in a chain of spasm. Our bodies thundered against each other, the rhythm became more fast and frantic causing an explosion inside me, releasing an animal instinct that I did not know I possessed. I bit his neck.

Making love as a vampire could not compare to anything he had made me felt before when I was human, every caress and every kiss had been intensified by the thousands, it was like being in uber-overdrive.

"Wow," I said.

He smiled proudly, "ditto."

I chuckled, "I love you Victor."

"I love you too," he gently touched my face, "You sure gave me a scare."

"I didn't mean too, I am sorry I doubted you."

"You doubted me?"

"Yes, I thought you had killed me." I grinned slightly.

He looked upset, "there is no way I can live without you. I thought you knew that," he lay back down and placed his hands behind his head to relax.

"I'm convinced now." I rested my head on his chiseled tone chest.

I continued, "--you're never going to guess who I saw," I raised my head to gaze at him.

He snickered, "what are you talking about? Who did you see?" He asked incredulously.

"My mom... she sent me back to you and the twins."

"You saw her? Where did you go?"

"I think that was heaven. She still fond of you, she has seen the twins too."

"Huh, I guess you are one of the lucky ones," he grinned.

"But I won't see her anymore," I said saddened.

He kissed me on the cheek, "you have us now."

"Victor, if you had taken the vial of poisoned blood, what would have happened? Do vampires go to heaven?"

"I don't know, I don't think so... I have heard older vampires say that there is an afterlife for vampires, where we are supposed to go back to our previous life before we became vampires and as punishment we are unable to remember anything from our life as a vampire, others say that you are in a purgatory with no one around --- but those are just tales."

"But how could not remembering all the bad sadistic stuff you have done as a vampire, be a punishment?"

"Because there you will not be reunited with your loved ones, supposedly you spent purgatory by yourself without any family member ---our afterlife is not like heaven." He explained.

"How about the other vampires wouldn't they all end up there?"

"You would think so, but since we don't normally die, and I guess if we did, we would not remember anything, —you would be one confused vampire living in solitude," he snickered.

"Oh, I see," I shivered, troubled by his fable tale, "no wonder vampires are so indestructible."

"I know the thought of it is creepy, right? ---going to a place that there is no past, is scary isn't it?" He grinned flashing his teeth trying to intimidate me. "It's all a myth, one that we will never need to prove wrong."

"But what if it is true, you wouldn't be able to remember me."

"Don't worry, that will not happen," he paused, "there is no way I can forget you," he smiled.

I smiled, "I'm sure you are right, I don't think I could forget you either."

"Get dressed, I'll take you to see the twins and then we can grab something to drink."

We walked to the twins' room, each one slept in their white cribs with white tulle mesh canopy clouding over the cribs, a blue and a pink bow differentiated each one.

I gently kissed their heads.

On my way out of the room, I caught my reflection in the mirror. I looked the same but I was paler than before, I had a radiant glow, I noticed that my complexion was spotless and flawless, —no more pimples. I grinned, and noticed my fangs.

I then glanced at Victor who was standing by the door watching me.

His lips pursed, then he said, "You look the same as before, just perfectly beautiful," he blew me a kiss.

I walked to his side and wrapped my arms around his neck, "I love you, Victor. I don't ever want to lose you."

"And you won't," he put his arms around my waist, "together forever?"

"Yes, together forever." I kissed him.

"What do you say if we go on a trip to Italy, then France and Spain?"

I gasped, "Are you serious?"

"Yes," he gave me short sweet kisses on my lips, the same way he used to do when I was sixteen.

"I would love to… there are so many places in Europe I would love to visit."

"And you will, we have an eternity to travel and enjoy the world," he said.

I slowly dropped my arms. Something got my attention. "What is that smell?" I said alertly.

"That has to be Emma or Estella warming up their food."

"Food?"

"Blood… you are smelling blood."

"The smell is enticing …hard to resist," I gave him a puzzling look, "How were you able to restrain yourself from biting me?"

"Are you kidding it wasn't easy… probably one of the hardest things I have ever done."

I rushed downstairs following the delicious smell.

"Amber, welcome again to our family," Estella hugged me.

"Happy Birthday!" Max shouted.

They all laughed.

"Looking good… looking good for a new born, so you are one of us now, huh?" Max said.

"Yes, I do feel like a new born, ---I am learning and feeling new stuff, everything feels so new to me."

"You will catch up on quick," Mr. Cromwell said.

"She is hungry," Victor said.

"Of course, —especially after mating," Max said wittily.

Emma chuckled.

"Guys, stop!" Victor said to them.

I turned to Victor and whispered, "How do they know?"

He grinned, "There are certain things we can't hide, and that's one of them."

"Oh!" I exclaimed ashamed.

"And this is where she would blush, ---yeap, she is definitely not human," Estella laughed.

Victor hugged me, "Ok everyone leave her alone, she has to get used to her new life."

"Amber, do you want to go hunting?" Emma asked excited.

"Not yet," Victor answered quickly. "I want to be the one to teach her."

"Do you want some of what we are drinking?" Estella asked. "It will fill you up in the meantime."

"Sure it smells delicious."

Max laughed. "It might give you indigestion… I don't think you liked her much."

"Who?" I asked innocently.

"It's aged blood, we had it in the freezer for a couple of years… its uhm," Estella stopped mid sentence and glanced at Victor.

"It's from your friend Chloe," Emma blurted out.

"Eww! Her?" I turned to look at Victor. "Is that what happened to her?"

Victor nodded. "I didn't think you would care," he smiled wickedly.

"Oh I don't, but if I didn't like her in person, what makes you think I would like her blood now?"

He laughed, "you are the one saying that it smells delicious."

I pouted, "I'm just hungry that's all."

"Well we have other types of blood," Max looked inside the silver fridge, "we have fox, rabbit, deer and possibly elk if Aubrey hasn't finished it all and two packets of type B blood." Max looked at Victor, "you are running low bro."

I felt brave, "That's ok. I'll take a sip of that little wench."

Emma poured me some in a cup, "here you go. Cheers!"

"Bottoms up," I drank the whole thing. It was not what I was expecting. It was bland, just like I remembered her. "Yuk!" I complained.

Victor laughed.

I glanced at Max, "the fox blood sounds better."

"Fox blood coming right up," Max smiled.

"I'll take you hunting later in the evening, ---promise," Victor said.

"Thank you, I need to learn if I have to teach the twins."

"We will both teach them, we are a family now," Victor grinned proudly.

CHAPTER 15

Time passes slow when you do not sleep. I could not differ day from night, I was never tired.

The twins were eight months now, they were more active crawling and cruising around holding onto the furniture. Little Victor was more insecure than Savannah; she was more adventurous already taking a few steps on her own. They were also communicating with sounds and short little words, calling Victor 'da-da'. It was hard to believe that they were some type of hybrid vampire. They were too adorable.

I was in the room alone with them, I tried to feed them milk again, but they would wrinkle their noses in displeasure to the milk taste. Actually, it was grossing me out too.

"Stop feeding them that, I don't think they like it," Victor chuckled as he entered the room.

"I know, but I want them to grow healthy."

"Blood is healthy," Victor grinned and picked up little Savannah, blowing kisses on her stomach making her laugh.

"For us is ok, but do you think that is enough for them?" I smiled. I enjoyed seeing him play with the twins. We were just like any normal family with the exception of our diet and sleeping habits.

"I think you are worrying too much, and you should let life

take its course, if they are like us is ok."

I picked up little Victor from his high chair. Little Victor was getting impatient waiting for me to get him, "I guess so," I kissed his cold cheeks.

"Do you want me to fetch some fresh warm blood for them?" Victor asked.

"Sure why not."

Victor left to go hunt.

I wondered who was going to be the poor victim this time. I was a newborn vampire, but I still had traces of my human feelings, something that Victor would complain about, especially when we would go hunting. If the animal looked too adorable I had a hard time attacking it, but Victor told me that in time, those feeling will turn off completely, but right now I felt a bit sad for that poor soul.

I played peek-a-boo with the twins on their mat on the floor, but they were not as excited as usual. I guess they did need the nourishment from the blood, I bit my index finger and let each one take turns sucking on it.

Victor returned with two bottles filled with warm blood. "Who is hungry?" He sat with us on the floor.

We gave them the bottles, but they were not too hungry they only drank half of it, before they fell asleep and we put them on their cribs.

"How come they get to sleep and not us?" I asked envying their peaceful sleep.

"Because they are growing and developing inside, and we are already fully grown," Victor unscrewed the nipple cap from the bottle and drank the rest.

"Victor!" I reproached.

"What? You can expect me to let good blood go to waste."

"No... but the least you can do is share."

He snickered, "Sorry, sometimes I forget you aren't human anymore, but you still act like one, ---here there is still some left," he handed me the other bottle.

I drank it and smacked my lips, "What type of animal is this, it taste different very succulent?"

"I know," he gave me a wicked smile, "Its human... a hunter I found nearby."

"The taste is addictive."

"Sure is, and I want you to stay away from it," he said and walked downstairs to the kitchen to rinse the bottles.

I followed him, "Why? You are feeding it to the twins," I questioned.

"It is nutritious to them, --but to you it can make you more vicious, and I rather not see you that way."

"Ok, ---humans are off limits then." Anyways I did not feel I was capable of attacking someone, at least not yet.

Victor hugged me. "You sure have taken in the whole vampire thing very smoothly. I had some trouble with Emma. I couldn't keep her away from attacking humans, Aubrey and I had to lock her up, and chain her until she finally calmed down and after several months in isolation, she has been different."

"Really?"

He nodded, "Really… but you have been real good, so I don't think I have to lock you up."

"May be I was meant to be a vampire," I commented.

"No one is meant to be a vampire."

Emma and Max stumbled in laughing.

"What's going on?" Victor asked.

"Nothing," Emma bit her lips trying not to laugh.

"Your sister is crazy, that's all I got to say," Max grinned.

They both looked like they were on a high, sort of intoxicated.

A slight smell of blood was in the air.

"Have you guys been hunting?" Victor asked as he walked next to them smelling the fresh blood on their breath. He then stopped and with his penetrating hazel eyes gazed at them sternly.

Emma and Max immediately stood firmly and humorless, they both bow down their heads to Victor.

Victor paced fiercely in front of them. Victor had a ghastly expression on his face. His eyes had turn jet black.

It was an intense moment, even I felt frightened and submissive by Victor's demonic demeanor. He seemed to be scolding them, without saying a word.

"What is going on Victor?" Mr. Cromwell walked in.

"They made a wrong choice, ---but I think they should tell you, and when they are ready they can come to me," Victor slowly took his evil eyes away from them. "Come on Amber," Victor took me by the arm and we walked outside.

"What happened in there? What was that about?" I asked.

"Emma and Max went hunting," he looked agitated.

"So?" I shrugged my shoulders.

"They had human blood scent on them, not just one but a few."

"Oh."

"They hunted in the city."

"But didn't you kill a hunter earlier?"

"In the woods, where is normal that an animal can attack... not in the city," he said unsmiling.

"But how did you know?"

"I am their maker, I know these things."

In the distant, I could see Max walking toward us.

Victor swiftly turned around.

His vampire senses were keen, unlike mine.

Max reached us. "Amber would you excuse us, I would like to have a word with Victor, please?"

"Sure," I said.

"No... whatever you need to tell me, you can say it in front of her, she is my wife."

Max lowered his head in respect, "I... just wanted to apologize, I know what we did was wrong, I should have stopped her but I didn't."

"Was this Emma's idea?"

Max nodded, "Yes."

"I think is about time you both move away... far away from us. I don't want you guys calling attention to us and the twins. I just started my own family and I won't allow you and Emma to jeopardize our existence."

"Victor!" I said hoping he would change his mind.

"Shh," he quickly glanced at me, returning his stare to Max.

"I'll let her know," Max bowed his head and left.

"Victor, why?"

"They need to learn to be on their own, if they cannot follow my rules."

"But ---you are going to give them another chance, right?" I asked.

"No!" he said adamantly.

[177]

Victor was very solemn the rest of the day and night.

I went to see the twins in the morning. Each one was standing in their crib babbling.

"Good morning. How is my sweet little Victor," I picked him up.

"Ma-ma," he babbled.

"Yes, I am your mommy," I kissed him.

"How about you, can you say ma-ma?"

Savannah raised her little arms for me to pick her up.

"Let me help you with her," Emma had sneaked up behind me.

I turned, "I didn't hear you come in," I said.

"I wanted to say goodbye before we left… Max told me you were there when Victor made his decision."

"Yes… I tried to vouch for you guys, I even asked him to give you another chance." I gave her a disheartened shrug.

"Victor can be unyielding," Emma said mournfully.

"What happened, Emma? --Victor said you were different."

"I am, --what started as a harmless cat and mouse game for us, turned out bad for that family --I couldn't stop myself when I saw the boy fall and gash his leg on the park, —the smell of fresh blood brought back old memories, I don't know if he has told you I was addicted to human blood once."

I nodded, "Yes."

She said remorseful, "We killed the boy; we could not let the others get away. They had seen us and they were about to run away…"

"Did you explain that to Victor?"

She snickered, "No Victor can be ruthless."

"I don't want you to go, let me talk to him one more time."

"I don't think he'll change his mind, Amber. He doesn't care about us as he used to, we don't do anything fun anymore. Victor has changed a lot since the birth of the twins," she said regretfully.

"Don't say that, he is the same old Victor?" I assured.

She chuckled, "Yeah an old fuddy duddy."

I smiled, "Just talk to him."

Victor entered the twins' room. He sighed when he saw Emma there, "What are you doing here?"

"I am leaving don't worry… take care Amber," she then

kissed each of the twins. "Au revoir, Victor," Mockingly she bowed reverently saying goodbye in French.

"Emma, stop!" I handed the twins to Victor and went after her. "You are a fool. If she leaves I am not talking to you again," I said curtly.

He looked at me astounded.

I talked to Emma and with Estella's help, I convinced her to stay. Now I just needed to stand up to Victor.

Victor stood by the window looking outside. The twins were delightfully entertained on the swings.

"She is not leaving," I said feisty and closed the door. I leaned against the door waiting for him to bark at me.

"I know," he then turned.

I walked slowly toward him and stood facing him.

He sighed and shook his head.

"That's it? you are not going to argue?" I asked surprised.

He gazed at me, "How? I can't win with you," his lips pursed.

I smiled triumphantly, "Great! –let me tell her then."

"Wait, I'll tell her. I still have to show that I am the authority around here."

I grinned, "Of course --the alpha male. You are definitely our maker --but I wear the pants," I said teasing him.

He sneered, "You are pressing your luck missy. Just because I was being extortionate by a beautiful vampire doesn't mean I lost my manhood," he gave me a crooked smile. "Not a word of this to them, you hear?"

I smiled then I pressed my lips together, and made the motion that I was locking my lips shut.

Later that evening we all gathered like a big family in the living room, talking and laughing having a wonderful time, suddenly I noticed a change in the twins. They seemed exhausted, and withdrawn.

I picked up little Savannah and her body temperature had risen.

"Victor she is hot, is this normal?"

"No… I don't think so."

I saw panic in his eyes.

"Aubrey, please call Dr. Abendroth," he ordered.

The doctor and Olga had moved out of the house since my conversion to a vampire. They were living in a small house Victor had bought for them, not too far from our estate.

Estella picked up little Victor. "His body is hot too," she noticed.

"Let's take them upstairs quick," Victor said.

We undressed the twins, leaving them only in their underpants. I folded their worn clothes and left them on top of the dresser. We tried our best to keep the twins awake and cool, but they were lethargic and finally closed their eyes.

I was feeling antsy, —the doctor was taking too long to arrive. I rubbed my upper arms for comfort; I was heading to the point of desperation. I saw Max hug Emma.

Estella stood by me as we both stared at Victor pacing around like a caged animal waiting for the doctor to arrive.

I went to check on the twins, they were still sleeping like little angels. I slowly caress their forehead. The temperature had dropped on little Victor, then I touched Savannah's and hers had dropped too. Their little bodies were cool.

"Their temperature is dropping," I said excitedly to Victor.

Victor looked at me implausible. "How? Are they awake?"

"No they are still sleeping."

He rushed to touch them. He closed his eyes blood tears started rolling down his face.

"Why are you crying? I said concerned.

Victor would not answer.

"Look at me, dammed it." I pounded his chest. "Are they ok?"

Victor gulped taking in a deep breath, "I can't sense them."

"No… no… no," I shouted anguished.

Mr. Cromwell walked in with Dr. Abendroth.

Emma was crying too, Max was consoling her. Estella had blood tears rolling down her grief stricken face.

Victor hugged me, as I sobbed uncontrollably, blood tears ran down my face.

Dr. Abendroth checked their little stiff bodies.

"Are they really death Doctor?" My voice cracked.

"Yes."

"No… no," I shouted. "They are just sleeping, right? ---

please tell me they are." I shook their little bodies trying to wake them up, but nothing happened.

Victor and Max pulled me away.

"What happened, Victor? --please make them better."

"I can't sweetheart, I would if I could."

"How about you, Aubrey?" I asked Mr. Cromwell.

"They are gone, Amber. There is nothing we can do," Mr. Cromwell shook his head.

"Would you help me Aubrey?" Victor asked him.

Estella walked to the closet and pulled out two blankets.

I stood motionless watching them move around the room.

"What is that for?" I asked confused.

"We have to wrap them for the proper burial."

"So soon? No, Victor, let me stay with them a little longer, please," I begged him.

"Amber, they are not here, they are gone," he replied.

"Please, I am begging you, at least let me say goodbye."

"Ok."

They all left the room with him, and left me alone with the twins. I cuddled their little bodies. I kissed them and put them down on their crib, saying my last goodbye to my little Victor and Savannah. I kept wiping blood tears that were profusely running down my face. I had gotten some tears on them and I wiped clean their bodies, and dressed them up in some new outfits, Estella had gotten for them.

I grabbed their worn clothes from top of the dresser and clutched them against my chest, taking in their scent. I then walked out of their room, hugging their little dirty clothes against my chest. Feeling lost in my sorrow, my eyes filled with agonizing pain. I saw Victor standing in the hallway, I could not dare look at him, and as a ghost I walked by him.

He tried to hold me but I continued walking, no one could imagine the pain I was in. I went straight to our room and locked the door.

Estella knocked on the door, "Amber, are you coming?" She said from the other side of the door.

I was in a daze but I heard her, "No… I can't, --it's too much for me."

"I understand, I'll tell Victor."

I sat on the edge of the bed smelling their little clothes. I had lost my sense of living, the main reasons I had come back from heaven. I looked at the bookcase were I had seen Victor hide the vial containing the poisoned blood.

I found it in the same place, and set it on the antique night table, next to the lamp.

I then heard them outside and I walked toward the window. From there I could see where they were going to start the bonfire. Aubrey was holding the little body wrapped in pink and Victor was carrying the one wrapped in blue. They were gathered outside next to the pile of wood. Max, Estella and Emma were holding hands. Dr. Abendroth stood by them. Victor slowly walked and placed little Victor's body on the wooden platform they had quickly arranged, then he grabbed little Savannah from Aubrey's arms and placed her next to little Victor. He then moved back and looked up at the window where he saw me, his face covered with blood tears. He then gave the okay to Dr. Abendroth to proceed.

Dr. Abendroth then lighted the fire.

I watched in agony as the fire consumed their bodies. I pressed my forehead against the window glass, and blew them one last kiss. I could not stand the pain anymore. I grabbed a pen and paper from the desk, and wrote a quick note to Victor. *'Dear Victor, if our love is meant to be, we will meet on the other side. I will be waiting. Together forever, love Amber.'* I folded the piece of paper and left it next to the lamp.

I then walked back to the window to say goodbye to my new family.

Victor then turned around, looked up at the window, and watched intensively and then his stare turned to terror.

"I love you," I muttered hoping that he would hear me say it one last time.

I stepped back moving away from the window toward and grabbed the vial from the table, and sat on the bed.

"No, Amber!" I heard Victor scream coming from outside.

I opened the vial and drank it all. I was not strong enough to continue living this life even if I still had Victor. I was ready to move on to the unknown. I knew in my heart, that if he really loved me, he would do the same.

I could feel the poisoned blood burning me from the inside. I then closed my eyes and waited for the inevitable. I heard the door blast open.

Again I heard his voice one last time, "Amber no, what did you do?" Victor scooped me up. "Don't. Please don't," he cried.

I then appeared again at the dark tunnel, I was not sure if it was the same as before, this time I could not hear anyone calling out for me, so I left my heart guide me. I walked in the darkness until I finally reached the outside. Everything seemed peaceful, flowers and green pasture, even a waterfall.

I then saw a black baby stroller. I ran toward it, my white dress swayed in the breeze. Inside the stroller sat little Savannah and Victor dressed in their little white outfits, each one had a teddy bear, their cheeks were rosy, they were smiling. I cried tears of happiness, my babies were alive in this unknown place, but I did not care if this was the vampire purgatory as long as the twins were with me. I picked them up and squeezed them tight, I was not going to let them go. I then saw the projection of Victor against the white cloudy background.

He was sitting next to my body, crying uncontrollably, the note was clenched inside his fist.

Emma pulled him aside and talked to him.

Max and Aubrey wrapped my body in a blanket like a mummy.

I then saw Emma put something in Victor's hand. He then hugged her as if he was saying goodbye.

Estella came to hug him, then Aubrey, and Max followed by Dr. Abendroth who seemed to be crying.

I saw them leave the room.

Victor then sat back down next to my wrapped body. I saw what he had in his hand; it was the poisoned blood vial that belonged to Emma. I do not know if she gave it to him voluntarily or if he ordered her to give it to him, but one thing I knew for sure was that he was coming.

"Daddy is coming," I said to the twins and kissed their rosy cheeks.

He seemed to be hesitating. He stood up and walked around nervously for a while.

I knew he was making a difficult decision, but it was the right one. "Come on Victor, you can do it, for us please —we need you,"

I said softly.

He then finally opened it and stared at it for a moment. He seemed distraught and irritated. He sat down on the bed again, his hand was shaking, he looked around as if waiting for someone to stop him, and then he drank it. He lay down next to my wrapped body, and he closed his eyes, he seemed to be hurting, his body jerked in pain.

"Remember me please," I whispered before the projection of him disappeared.

"Daddy is coming. We just need to wait for him." I said excited.

I placed one of their little blankets on the floor and we waited for Victor.

I dozed off with them, and later woke up but Victor was not there yet. We waited and waited and Victor did not arrive. I could not understand why, he has to be dead, I saw him drink the poisoned blood. I waited longer it seemed like an eternity, the twins kept me company, I played with them. I had no idea as to how much time has passed, but little Savannah was walking and little Victor struggle a little but he was walking too.

I was getting tired of waiting for him. My hopes of seeing him again were fading. I wondered if I had made a mistake.

I took the twins for a stroll. Then I stopped in my tracks when I heard that unforgettable voice.

"Pardon me Miss."

It sounded different. It had an accent. I slowly turned around hoping that my imagination was not playing tricks on me.

I smiled when I saw his face. His hair was a little longer than before, but he looked the same dark brown hair, ivory skin, and beautiful hazel eyes. Just as I remembered, remarkably handsome and physically fit, the only thing different was that he was wearing all white. I gasped, "Hi."

"Hello, my name is Victor Antonio Cortez. ---I don't know if you can help me, but I seem to be lost," he chuckled.

My eyebrows furrow, I could feel my face tightening. Is he ok? I thought. Then a feeling of fear overwhelmed me, a horrible thought came to my head, the one thing I dreaded the most, he had forgotten. I gulped, "Who you are looking for?" I asked hoping he was teasing me.

"That I don't know, I was hoping to see my family, but I haven't seen anyone but you, I have been wandering around and I keep returning back to this same place where you are, —I feel like I am walking in circles."

"You have seen me here before?"

"Yes, I hide behind the trees and see you play with the little ones, but then I walk the other way."

"Why?" I still did not know if he was playing a prank on me, but if he was, he sure was being convincing.

"I didn't want to disturb you. You seemed to be waiting for someone."

The twins started babbling. "Da-Da."

I lowered my gaze to where the twins were playing with their teddy bears, and then I turned my eyes on Victor who was staring at them too.

"Are they yours Miss? ---sorry perhaps I should call you madam," he chuckled.

"It doesn't matter what you call me, my name is Amber," I said with a sad grimace. I was brokenhearted at the thought that he had not remembered me, he was not playing —what he had told me about this place was true.

"Amber, that is a beautiful name," he said with his Spaniard accent. "Are you also looking for your family?"

"Not anymore, I have found mine," I said sadly.

He walked closer to look at the twins, "they are precious, what are their names?"

"This is Savannah and this is..." I paused, "uhm Victor, —he is named after his father." I waited to see if that would jolt his memories.

Victor snickered, "now, that's a coincidence!"

Savannah babbled, "Da-Da."

"She is cute," he smiled at her.

I could not hold in my insecurities anymore. I needed to know. "You don't remember us, do you?"

He looked puzzled, "Should I?"

"Yes, ---we are your family," I said with a tone of annoyance.

"Sorry madam, but you must be confused," he shook his head.

"Why do you think you keep coming back to this place? You

are looking for us," I was losing my patience. I needed him to remember us —he had to.

"Don't you think I would know if you were my family?"

"Look, you are wearing your wedding ring, and so am I, they are the same," I showed him my wedding band, and said, "I have been waiting here for you."

He shook his head disconcerted, running his fingers through his hair, and then said, "I am sorry but I must go madam, I can't stay here, someone is out there waiting for me."

I grabbed his arm, "please Victor try to remember how much I love you, and how much you said you loved me and that our love was eternal, —can you please remember that?" I rambled desperately. I looked into his hazel eyes, hoping to see a ray of my old Victor still alive inside, "you are supposed to meet me and the kids, —you have to remember us. You swore to me, you would never forget me." Tears rolled down my face. My heart was aching knowing that he wanted to leave us again.

He sighed. "If what you are telling me is the truth, why can't I remember?" He said frustrated and looked at me as if I was crazy.

I could not tell him why, I did not have the heart, and besides if I did, that would only prove what he was already thinking of me. Then I did the first thing that came to my mind, surely it had to work, I thought. "Kiss me," I said eagerly.

"I beg your pardon?"

I grabbed his face. I pressed my lips against his, and forcedly kissed him. The kiss was fierce and I ravished his mouth.

He pushed me away, "Madam, please control yourself!" His cheeks turned red.

I took a step back, and looked at him defeated, all I had was that kiss. I had nothing else to prove to him that he belonged with us. I had no other way to convince him that he was and will always be my true love. I slowly dropped on my knees succumbed by the grief I was feeling, more tears rolled down my face, I could not stop crying, I covered my face. I had failed, —I had lost him.

Shortly after the kiss, he seemed to be in some sort of a trance, he stood by in silence, he had nothing to say and neither did I.

Then he kneeled down in front of me, "my precious Amber, I am sorry I didn't mean to make you cry," the tone of his voice was different. It was sweet and loving just like before.

I lifted up my head, and with my eyes welled up with tears, I looked at him surprised, "You called me Amber." I whimpered.

His piercing eyes looked deeply into mine, "my precious Amber," he repeated.

"You remembered," I sobbed. I felt as if my heart started to beat again with joy.

"Vaguely," he looked sadly at the twins in the stroller. He then tenderly touched my face wiping off the tears. "I think I remember the first time I saw you, ---and how I felt the first time I touched your face," he paused. His eyes gleamed and he continued, "you mean a lot to me, don't you?"

I sniffed, "Yes, we are soul mates." I nodded and smiled.

"That would explain the sudden surge of feelings I am experiencing right now."

"Our love is pure and eternal," I said in a soft soothing tone trying to reassure him that what he was feeling was real.

"So we are meant to be together?" He gave me a soft seductive smile.

"Yes." I smiled. My dreams were coming back to life, my happily forever after was within reach. I continued to tell him a little bit more about our previous life together, but I did not get into details as to what he was and what he had done to me. He deserved to be happy and it was about time I found happiness again.

"How about them, I don't remember them?" He looked at the twins with his eyes glassy with tears. Then a teardrop appeared on the corner of his eye.

I finally got to see him with real tears; he was as human as me and the twins.

"They are your blood and you will learn to love them, I saw how you smiled at Savannah." I reassured him.

He smiled, his eyes were on me, he would not look away and he carefully studied my face, taking a mental picture that I hoped he would never forget.

"Victor, all that I ask of you know is to remember the love we have for each other, nothing more nothing less." I caressed his face and he leaned toward my touch.

He seemed to be remembering more. A pleasant smile appeared on his face as snip-its from our previous life were resurfacing in his mind. He still looked somewhat disoriented, but that did not stop him, and he told me what I waited this long to hear, "I love you Amber."

His captivated gaze held my attention, and made me feel warm inside. I could not blink, "I love you too Victor, always."

He then leaned closer, "together forever," he muttered, before his mouth descended on mine, and filled my lips with soft butterfly kisses.

About the Author

Judith is a single mother of three boys, and recently became the proud grandmother of a beautiful baby girl. She lives in Houston, Texas with her two younger sons, and their two rescued dogs. In between her full time job and daily motherly duties, she is able to squeeze time in her busy schedule to write young adult fantasy and paranormal romance novels. Her debut book, *The Girl Without A Past*, a Middle Grade novel was released in October 2011 by Copperhill Media.

To find out more about Judith and her other novels, visit her website.

Author's Website
www.judithpvaughan.com

Made in the USA
Charleston, SC
18 January 2012